*Chloe made Donovan feel special—
almost like a man who deserved a
woman like her.*

No way could he resist the temptation of her kiss.
Just for a moment, he promised himself.

But with one taste, he was lost.

He tried to remind himself that Chloe was
endowing him with qualities he didn't possess.
That she was turning him into some kind of hero
because they had grown to depend on each other
during their kidnapping ordeal. Yet with her kiss,
he found it all too easy to believe she wanted him
for exactly who he was, flaws and all.

That sort of self-deception was dangerous. He'd
never indulged in it before.

But everything was different with Chloe. She
tempted him in ways he'd never been tempted
before.

She almost tempted him to forget she was the
woman his best friend planned to marry....

Dear Reader,

April may bring showers, but it also brings in a fabulous new batch of books from Silhouette Special Edition! This month treat yourself to the beginning of a brand-new exciting royal continuity, CROWN AND GLORY. We get the regal ball rolling with Laurie Paige's delightful tale *The Princess Is Pregnant!* This romance is fair to bursting with passion and other temptations.

I'm pleased to offer *The Groom's Stand-In* by Gina Wilkins— a fascinating story that is sure to keep readers on the edge of their seats…and warm their hearts in the process. Peggy Webb is no stranger herself to heartwarming romance with the next installment of her miniseries THE WESTMORELAND DIARIES. In *Force of Nature,* a beautiful photojournalist encounters a primitive man in the wilderness and must find a way to tame his oh-so-wild heart.

In *The Man in Charge*, Judith Lyons gives us a tender reunion romance where an endangered chancellor's daughter finds herself being guarded by the man she's never been able to forget—a rugged mercenary who's about to learn he's the father of their child! And in Wendy Warren's new sensation *Dakota Bride,* readers will relish the theme of learning to love again, as a young widow dreams of love and marriage with a handsome stranger. In addition, you'll find an intriguing case of mistaken identity in Jane Toombs's *Trouble in Tourmaline*, where a world-weary lawyer takes a breather from his fast-paced life and finds his sights brightened by a lovely psychologist, who takes him for a gardener. You won't want to put this story down!

So kick back and enjoy the fantasy of falling in love, and be sure to return next month for another winning selection of emotionally satisfying and uplifting stories of love, life and family!

Best,

Karen Taylor Richman
Senior Editor

Please address questions and book requests to:
Silhouette Reader Service
U.S.: 3010 Walden Ave., P.O. Box 1325, Buffalo, NY 14269
Canadian: P.O. Box 609, Fort Erie, Ont. L2A 5X3

The Groom's Stand-In

GINA WILKINS

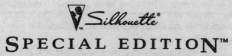

SPECIAL EDITION™

Published by Silhouette Books

America's Publisher of Contemporary Romance

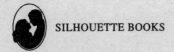 **SILHOUETTE BOOKS**

ISBN 0-373-24460-6

THE GROOM'S STAND-IN

Copyright © 2002 by Gina Wilkins

Books by Gina Wilkins

Silhouette Special Edition

The Father Next Door #1082
It Could Happen to You #1119
Valentine Baby #1153
†*Her Very Own Family* #1243
†*That First Special Kiss* #1269
Surprise Partners #1318
**The Stranger in Room 205* #1399
**Bachelor Cop Finally
    Caught?* #1413
**Dateline Matrimony* #1424
The Groom's Stand-In #1460

†Family Found: Sons & Daughters
**Hot off the Press
§Family Found
‡The Family Way

**Previously published
as Gina Ferris**

Silhouette Special Edition

Healing Sympathy #496
Lady Beware #549
In from the Rain #677
Prodigal Father #711
§*Full of Grace* #793
§*Hardworking Man* #806
§*Fair and Wise* #819
§*Far To Go* #862
§*Loving and Giving* #879
Babies on Board #913

**Previously published
as Gina Ferris Wilkins**

Silhouette Special Edition

‡ *A Man for Mom* #955
‡*A Match for Celia* #967
‡*A Home for Adam* #980
‡*Cody's Fiancée* #1006

Silhouette Books

Mother's Day Collection 1995
Three Mothers and a Cradle
"Beginnings"

GINA WILKINS

is a bestselling and award-winning author who has written more than fifty novels for Harlequin and Silhouette Books. She credits her successful career in romance to her long, happy marriage and her three "extraordinary" children.

A lifelong resident of central Arkansas, Ms. Wilkins sold her first book to Harlequin in 1987 and has been writing full-time since. She has appeared on the Waldenbooks, B. Dalton and *USA Today* bestseller lists. She is a three-time recipient of the Maggie Award for Excellence, sponsored by Georgia Romance Writers, and has won several awards from the reviewers of *Romantic Times*.

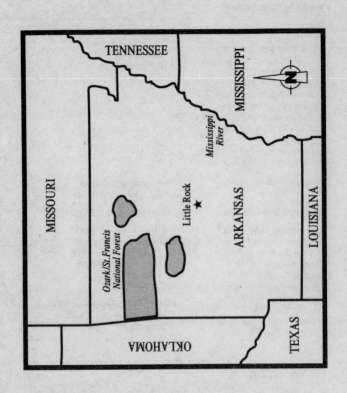

Chapter One

Donovan Chance had done a lot of favors for his friend and employer, Bryan Falcon—some involving actual risk to life and limb—but he had never served as a babysitter. While that wasn't exactly what he was doing on this Sunday afternoon in early April, the description felt uncomfortably accurate.

He had reluctantly agreed to escort Chloe Pennington—Bryan's current girlfriend—from her Little Rock, Arkansas, apartment to Bryan's vacation home on Table Rock Lake in southwest Missouri. It would be a little more than three hours in the car with a total stranger, a trip Donovan wasn't anticipating with any enthusiasm.

With a sigh, he reached for the door handle. He owed Bryan a lot more than a few favors—regardless of his personal feelings about this one in particular.

The apartment he'd been directed to was on the

ground floor, opening onto a covered sidewalk. Rain was in the forecast—lots of it—and the air was nippy. Hunching a little against a brisk breeze, he rang the doorbell.

From the photograph Bryan had shown him, he immediately recognized the woman who opened the door. Medium-brown hair cut in a smooth bob to her collar. Large, long-lashed hazel eyes set in a fair-skinned oval face. Straight, smallish nose. Soft mouth, the lower lip fuller than the top. More pretty than beautiful. Dressed very casually in jeans and a long-sleeved red T-shirt.

He wouldn't have thought she was Bryan's type—but then, this whole situation had been a surprise to him. He wished he could say it had been a pleasant one.

He was quite sure no emotions were revealed in his expression when he introduced himself. "Ms. Pennington? I'm Donovan Chance, Bryan Falcon's associate."

Rather than make him feel welcome, as he'd expected, she gave him a cool once-over that left him feeling like something she'd spotted floating in her soup. "Associate?" she asked. "Don't you mean flunky?"

His eyes narrowed in response to the unveiled insult. *This* was the woman Bryan wanted to marry? The one he'd described as sweet, warm, funny, a little old-fashioned? If Donovan hadn't seen a photograph, he would be certain he'd come to the wrong apartment. "You *are* Ms. Pennington, aren't you?" he asked just to be sure.

"Yes. May I call you Donnie?" Her honeyed tone was pure insolence this time. Donovan had always believed that no one could deliver an insult more effectively than a woman of the South.

"Not if you want me to answer." He hadn't been prepared to like her particularly, but he'd thought she'd at least make a show of being pleasant. He'd bet she never talked this way in front of Bryan. He'd had a great deal of experience dealing with difficult people, so he was able to keep his voice blandly polite. "I suppose we should get on the road. May I carry your bags for you?"

From babysitter to bellhop. Bryan could well owe *him* a few favors after this. Especially if Ms. Pennington's attitude didn't improve significantly. Soon.

"If it were up to me, no one would be getting in a car with you," she said, and her expression now seemed to be an odd mixture of frustration and disapproval. "Then your rich boss could go shopping elsewhere for a suitable partner for his ridiculous marriage of convenience."

Now he *was* confused. He'd thought Chloe Pennington was a willing participant in this whirlwind courtship—too willing, actually. He'd been certain she was as attracted to Bryan's money and power as to Bryan himself—as too many other women had been during the past few years. But this woman wasn't even pretending to be looking forward to the week she would be spending with the man who had been courting her so persistently. Did she really think it didn't matter how she spoke to Bryan's closest associate, as long as she behaved properly in front of Bryan himself?

Because he'd long since appointed himself Bryan's protector, he spoke sharply, "Look, if that's the way you really feel about this, let's just forget it. Bryan doesn't have time for a vacation now, anyway, especially with someone who would rather be elsewhere. And to be honest, I have plenty more important things to do than babysit a..."

"Grace? I saw Mrs. Callahan in the laundry room, and she asked me to tell you..." The woman who had entered the room, wearing khaki slacks and a mint-green sweater and carrying a load of folded laundry in a round plastic basket, came to an abrupt stop when she saw Donovan standing in the open doorway. "Oh," she said, looking suddenly flustered. "You must be Donovan Chance. You're early."

Donovan wasn't usually caught completely off guard, but it took him a moment to respond. "Actually, I'm exactly on time."

The woman set the laundry basket on the couch and approached the door. "I'm so sorry. My watch must have stopped again. It's been doing that lately."

Though their appearance was almost identical—the only difference being that this woman wore her brown hair slightly longer and straighter—the newcomer's voice was warmer than the one who had opened the door to him, her expression friendlier. "Grace, haven't you even invited Mr. Chance inside?"

"Actually, I had almost convinced him to leave without you." Her face resigned, Grace stepped out of Donovan's way.

Sighing, Chloe stepped forward to extend her hand in Donovan's direction. "I'm sorry if my sister was rude. Perhaps we should start from the beginning. I'm Chloe Pennington, and it's very nice to meet you, Mr. Chance. Bryan has often spoken of you."

Donovan remembered now that Bryan had mentioned that Chloe owned a business with her sister.

He had neglected to add that the sisters were identical twins. Donovan would have to discuss that with his friend later.

He shook Chloe's hand briefly. "It's nice to meet you, Ms. Pennington," he said, because etiquette demanded it of him.

"Please call me Chloe. And you've already met my sister, Grace."

Meeting Grace's glittering hazel eyes, Donovan nodded. "Yes, I've had that pleasure."

She flashed him a challenging smile.

Looking suspiciously from one to the other, Chloe shook her head. "Now I'm even more convinced that an apology for my sister's behavior must be in order."

Turning his back on Grace, Donovan looked at Chloe—the woman Bryan had chosen, he reminded himself. "Are you ready to leave?"

Chloe glanced at her watch, shook her wrist, then slipped it off and tossed it to her sister. "See if you can have that repaired while I'm gone, will you?"

Catching it easily, Grace replied, "You could always stay and see to it yourself."

"Don't start with me again." Chloe picked up the laundry basket and turned toward the doorway that led to the back of the apartment. "Five minutes," she promised Donovan. "Make yourself comfortable in the meantime."

He nodded, watching Grace a bit warily out of the corner of his eye.

Maybe Chloe sensed his uneasiness. "Grace, why don't you come help me get everything ready," she said, and her tone made it clear it wasn't a suggestion.

"I'm sure Mr. Chance won't mind waiting by himself for a few minutes."

"Not at all," he assured her.

Grace crossed her arms over her chest. "You can handle everything in there. I'll keep Falcon's chauffeur company."

Donovan was going to let it pass, but Chloe spoke sharply on his behalf. "Mr. Chance isn't a chauffeur, he's an executive in Bryan's company. He's doing Bryan a big favor by giving me a lift today because Bryan was detained in New York."

"An executive. Is that what they're calling errand boys these days?"

"Grace!"

Holding up a hand toward Chloe, Donovan focused on her sister. "You might as well get it off your chest. What other insults would you like to throw at me before I leave?"

He was a bit surprised to see her blush. She kept her chin high, defiance overcoming embarrassment. "I suppose I should apologize for the things I've said to you. You're only doing your job, I guess. It's my sister who needs some sense knocked into her."

"You don't approve of the engagement?"

"Bryan and I aren't engaged," Chloe said quickly. "We're still in the preliminary stage of our relationship. That's why we're taking some private time at his vacation home this week—to discuss the future in private. We were both disturbed when the press got wind of our friendship and started dropping hints about a possible marriage."

Grace whirled toward Donovan. "Do *you* approve of this ridiculous arrangement?"

He shrugged. No way, of course, was he going to

admit that he agreed with Grace Pennington—about anything. "It's none of my business."

"So you *are* just an employee and not a real friend of Bryan Falcon."

His eyes narrowed at that. "Bryan Falcon is the best friend I've ever had. But I don't tell him how to run his personal life."

Which didn't mean he wouldn't give his opinion when asked, of course. And if Bryan asked him, Donovan was going to suggest that his friend think a lot longer before making himself a part of *this* family.

"I wish you would teach that trick to my sister," Chloe said. "Not getting involved in other people's business, I mean."

Donovan doubted that there was anything Grace Pennington would be willing to learn from him. "We'd better get going," he said to Chloe, looking pointedly at his own efficiently accurate watch.

"I'll hurry," she replied. "Come on, Grace."

With a show of reluctance, Grace followed her twin from the room, leaving Donovan to exhale slowly and wonder what on earth Bryan had gotten the two of them into this time.

Strapped into a luxuriously soft and comfortable leather seat, Chloe looked through her lashes at the man behind the wheel of the expensive sedan. The passing scenery was lovely. Though it was a bit chilly due to a midnight rainstorm the night before, the past couple of weeks had been quite warm, coaxing new leaves from trees and bringing out daffodils, Bradford pear blossoms, and a few early azaleas. As much as she enjoyed the first signs of spring, Chloe found herself unable to stop surreptitiously studying her driver.

Bryan had described his second-in-command as the classic "strong, silent type"—tough, blunt-spoken, ruthless when necessary. He had then added that Donovan Chance was the most honest, loyal, reliable friend he'd ever had. Chloe had expected to be a little awkward with Donovan. She hadn't anticipated that she would be totally intimidated by him.

He wasn't as handsome as Bryan—not in the traditional sense, anyway. Donovan's features were more rugged than Bryan's. She would bet he'd had his nose broken in his youth; just enough to keep it from being perfectly straight. His jaw was square, his cheekbones broad, and his unsmiling eyes were such a pale, cool green they looked almost metallic. Nice mouth—but she doubted those firm, intriguingly etched lips curved into a smile very often.

He wore "business-casual" clothing—a thin, V-necked cream-colored sweater over a navy-and-cream checked shirt with navy chinos and loafers—but he looked as though he'd be more at home in a denim shirt, jeans and a pair of boots. He'd apparently made an effort to comb his medium-length, chestnut-brown hair into a conservative style, but it showed a tendency to tumble rebelliously onto his forehead.

On anyone else, she might have referred to that errant lock as "boyish." But not this guy. There was nothing boyish about Donovan Chance.

Because she knew that Donovan was Bryan's best friend as well as his employee, and since she figured she'd be spending a lot of time around him in the future if she and Bryan did marry, she decided that now was as good a time as any to try to get to know him. After all, that had been Bryan's intention when he'd sent Donovan to escort her to the resort, though she had assured him she was perfectly capable of traveling alone.

"Bryan told me you and he have known each other since high school," she said to kick off the conversation.

Donovan replied without taking his eyes off the road ahead. "Yeah."

"Were you neighbors?"

"No."

Okay, no more questions that could be answered in monosyllables, she decided. Whether he was just naturally averse to small talk, or was still smarting from Grace's rudeness, she didn't know, but they would never get anywhere this way. "How did you and Bryan meet?"

After a rather lengthy pause, he said, "Four guys were doing their best to beat me to a pulp. Bryan jumped in to help me."

Chloe felt her eyebrows rise as she tried to picture always-immaculate, elegant Bryan Falcon engaged in a vicious fist fight. On the other hand, she had no trouble at all imagining Donovan taking on four challengers. "Did you and Bryan win the fight?"

"Actually, they beat us both to a pulp."

Chloe was startled into a laugh. "That's terrible."

What might have been a smile—it was hard to tell with this man—quirked one corner of his mouth. "We recovered."

"So you and Bryan have been friends ever since?"

Another long pause—followed by another monosyllable. "Yeah."

Chloe stifled a sigh and sat back in her seat. Looked as though this was going to be a long, quiet trip. She might as well enjoy the view.

* * *

It was with effort that Donovan kept his gaze focused on the road ahead instead of the woman sitting in the passenger seat. Something about her kept drawing his attention her way.

A sideways glance let him see that she was gazing out the side window at the passing landscape, a somber look on her face. Her fingers were twisted in her lap so tightly that her knuckles gleamed. She didn't give the appearance of a woman on her way to a romantic getaway with the man she was planning to marry. Which made him wonder again why she was going along with this very businesslike courtship.

The most logical answer, of course, was that she had several million reasons—all green.

He was lousy at small talk, but he searched for something to say, a way to get her talking again so he could try to figure her out. "Bryan told me you're in the retail business."

She seemed relieved to be drawn out of her thoughts, even with such a lame conversational gambit. "Yes, Grace and I own a shop in Little Rock's River Market district. We call it Mirror Images—a shameless play on our being twins, I'll admit. We specialize in decorating accessories—unusual mirrors, mostly, but also pottery and sculpture, candleholders, carved boxes, blown-glass pieces. Many of the items are handmade and one-of-a-kind."

Hearing the enthusiasm in her voice, he could tell her heart was in her work. Bryan had always said that no business could be successful if the owner had no passion. It was probably Chloe's enthusiasm for her shop that had drawn Bryan to her in the first place. And maybe her smile…

He cleared his throat rather forcefully. "How's business? Making a profit?"

Her eyebrows rose. "We're doing all right," she said, her tone a bit cool now.

Did she think he'd gotten too nosy? Or did she simply not want to admit that the shop wasn't making money? He knew how difficult it was for a small business to survive. More than half folded within their first year of operation. It required a good deal of start-up capital to acquire stock, hire competent employees, purchase enough advertising to catch the buying public's attention....

He shrugged. "You'll do better once Bryan's involved."

Everyone knew that Bryan Falcon had an almost magical way of making every business he backed turn a sizeable profit. Donovan was sure Chloe was well aware of her new boyfriend's business talents—not to mention his notorious talent for charming women.

When she spoke this time, her tone was almost cool enough to deposit ice on his eyelashes. "I don't expect Bryan to be involved with my business in any way. My sister and I are perfectly capable of running it on our own."

"I see," he said—which didn't mean he believed her, of course. There was no way he'd accept that the financial advantages of marriage to one of the most successful venture capitalists in the country had never crossed her mind.

She frowned at him. "You think I'm only interested in Bryan's money?"

"I didn't say that."

"No—you didn't say it." But apparently, she'd interpreted his words that way anyway. She sat back in her seat, her face turned away from him, her posture stiff enough to let him know she'd taken offense.

He thought about trying to apologize, but decided to let it go. For one thing, he was lousy at apologies— hadn't made enough of them to get good at it. For another—well, hell, of *course* he figured she was interested in Bryan's money. He'd met few women— or men, for that matter—who weren't. And since her own sister had made it clear she didn't consider this a love match, then Chloe had to have more prosaic reasons for considering marriage to Bryan.

An eminently practical man himself, Donovan supposed he couldn't blame Chloe for keeping her eyes on the bottom line, but he still didn't approve of this whole arrangement. Bryan deserved better than to be married for his money.

Donovan believed his friend was overreacting to his last failed romantic relationship. Bryan had been burned by a woman who had convinced him that she wanted him for himself, not his money. The truth of that ruse had been revealed when she'd gone ballistic at the first mention of the rather strict prenuptial agreement that Bryan's team of attorneys had drafted years earlier. She hadn't been a good enough actress to convince anyone that the extent of her outrage couldn't be measured in dollar signs.

Because it hadn't been the first time Bryan had been deceived, he had come to the conclusion that the only way he could be certain of a potential mate's motives was to have everything spelled out from the beginning. He wanted children, and he wanted to raise them in a conventional two-parent family. He'd decided he should approach marriage the same way he started a new business—with legal contracts, long-term planning, calculated risks and clearly defined benefits.

Donovan had tried to point out that one didn't choose a wife the same way one hired a financial officer, but Bryan had shrugged off the admonition. To him, it had seemed like a perfectly logical plan.

He'd told Donovan about the day in February when he had wandered into Chloe's shop while on a break from a day-long meeting being held nearby. They'd started talking, then had somehow ended up having coffee together at the popular River Market pavilion. Bryan claimed to have known very quickly that Chloe was exactly the sort of woman he'd been searching for since he'd made the decision a few months earlier to enter into a practical marriage.

Donovan had never been accused of being even remotely romantic, but Bryan's plan seemed too cold and calculated even for him. He couldn't help wondering if someday Bryan was going to feel that he'd settled for less than he could have had, if he would always be aware that something important was missing.

Since he himself had no strong desire to reproduce, Donovan figured his way was easier—he didn't plan to marry anyone. Any relationships he entered into were strictly short-term and no-strings, so motives didn't really matter.

He was convinced that his strategy was the most practical of all.

They'd been on the road for almost an hour when Donovan realized that Chloe's posture was still unnaturally rigid. Her hands were still laced tightly together, her short pink nails digging into skin.

"Are you okay?" he couldn't resist asking. "My driving isn't making you nervous or anything, is it?"

His question brought her head around. "Of course not. You seem to be an excellent driver. I'm not nervous about anything at all."

Definitely a lie, he decided, glancing again at her telltale hands. "You just seemed a little tense."

"I'm fine." She looked straight ahead again as she spoke. "What is it you do in Bryan's organization, exactly?"

He shrugged. "Whatever he needs me to do."

"Such as escorting me today?"

Since the answer to that seemed obvious, he allowed it to pass.

"You've been out of the country for the past few months," she tried again. "In...Italy?"

"Venice. I was there for almost three months."

"That must have been very nice."

"It was business."

She twisted in her seat, tugging at the seat belt to allow her to look at him more closely. "Surely you took some time off for sightseeing."

"Not much," he admitted. "I was only supposed to be over there a couple of weeks. Problems kept cropping up to detain me. I was just trying to get everything settled so I could get back to the States."

"You must have missed your family."

"I don't have family. I had a lot of work piling up here that I needed to attend to."

"I see." She settled back into her seat again.

Because he knew Bryan wanted him to keep Chloe entertained, Donovan tried to think of something interesting to say about his weeks in Venice. "The food was good."

"I'm sure it was."

"And the sunrises were nice," he added. "I had a balcony, and I would sit out there and have coffee early in the mornings while I read through paperwork."

The enthusiasm of her response to that made him glad he'd gone to the extra conversational effort. "That must have been spectacular!" She lifted her clasped hands to her chest as she apparently tried to visualize the scene he'd described so sparingly. "I've always wanted to travel. To see some of the places I've only read about until now."

"When you marry Bryan, you'll be able to travel as much as you want." As he was sure she was aware.

She lowered her hands slowly to her lap. "*If* I marry Bryan," she corrected him, her voice a bit cool again.

"The gossip columnists seem to think it's all been decided." And he imagined the rumors were correct. Despite her affront at implications that she would marry Bryan for his money, why *wouldn't* she want to marry a multimillionaire who could take her to all those places she'd always wanted to visit?

She wrinkled her nose. "That's something I'm still having trouble getting used to—being in the gossip columns, I mean."

He shrugged again. "You'd better get used to it. For some reason, people seem to be fascinated with Bryan. Everything he does makes the papers."

Money, he thought, had a way of drawing attention. Combine a lot of money with Bryan's good looks, impressive family background, unerringly shrewd business decisions, personal charisma and single status, and the result was that he was included on every Most Eligible Bachelor list published in North America.

Just the hint that Bryan's name might soon be removed from those lists had the gossips all abuzz with curiosity, despite Bryan's efforts to keep his personal life private. Someone had apparently tipped off the tabloids about his interest in Chloe, much to Bryan's displeasure.

That was another reason Bryan had asked Donovan to play escort on this trip. He'd been concerned that Chloe might find herself annoyed by reporters. Donovan rarely had that problem. For some reason, they took one look at him and quietly put away their notebooks.

"One of the so-called reporters called me Zoe," Chloe muttered, "and another said it was Grace that Bryan's been seeing."

Donovan wondered if her disgruntled tone was because she'd been in the papers at all—or because they hadn't gotten her name right. "The way your sister was talking earlier, I doubt that she appreciated seeing her name linked with Bryan's," was all he said.

Chloe winced. "No, she didn't."

"What does she have against Bryan, anyway?" Maybe Grace was jealous that *she* wasn't the one poised to marry a multimillionaire.

"It isn't Bryan, exactly. She's just worried that I'm making a mistake. Grace has a little trouble trusting people—especially wealthy, powerful men. She's convinced herself I'm going to end up bitter and humiliated. Unlike *some* people," she added pointedly, "my sister knows I want more from a marriage than financial security, and she doesn't believe I can find those things with Bryan."

"And why is that?"

"She suspects that Bryan is playing me for a fool, and that he has no intention of settling down and raising a family."

"Bryan does what he says he'll do."

"You're very loyal to him."

Because she could never understand how much he owed Bryan—and because it wasn't any of her concern, anyway—he let the comment pass without remark.

They fell quiet again then. Donovan had run out of things to say, and Chloe seemed to have relaxed, if only marginally. Or perhaps even riding in uneasy silence seemed preferable to making stilted conversation with him.

He supposed he couldn't blame her for that.

Chapter Two

They'd been on the road for almost two hours when Donovan nodded toward a small convenience store ahead. "We're just past the halfway point of our trip. I could use a cold drink. How about you?"

"A cold drink sounds good."

He flipped on his turn signal, automatically glancing in the rearview mirror as he did so. A big, extended-cab pickup was right on his back bumper, followed by a blue, soccer-mom minivan. The van had its signal on, too—no surprise, since there wasn't another convenient place to stop for several miles ahead.

Because his gas tank was still more than half full, he drove into a parking space on one side of the small store. The only open space available, it lay in deep shadow. Though it wasn't a particularly cold day, Donovan felt a chill go through him when he turned off the motor. He'd learned to trust feelings like that;

he looked around before opening his door. Everything looked fine—a couple of older-model vehicles, several work-weary pickup trucks, and the soccer-mom van, which was parked at one of the three gas pumps.

Chloe eyed him quizzically. "Are you supposed to be my bodyguard?"

That whipped his head around, his eyes narrowing as he stared at her. "What makes you ask that?"

"Something about the way you checked out the place just now—all tense and alert, like a Hollywood version of a secret service agent."

His reply was more curt than he had intended. "I'm no bodyguard. Do you want to go in with me or wait out here?"

She reached for her door handle. "I'll go in."

He followed close on her heels as they stepped out of the shadows and around to the front of the store. She glanced over her shoulder at him when they entered. "If you'll excuse me a moment," she said, motioning in the general direction of the restrooms.

He nodded and turned to a wall-size cooler filled with soft drinks. He found himself watching the restroom doors during the brief time Chloe was out of his sight, though he couldn't imagine why he was suddenly so antsy.

This whole situation probably had him unnerved. Bryan was supposed to be making this trip, but he'd been detained in New York and had arranged to meet them at his Ozarks vacation home. He'd asked Donovan to make sure Chloe got there safely. In a couple of hours, Bryan would become Chloe's companion, and Donovan could get back to his own life—which, admittedly, consisted mostly of work.

Chloe joined him at the cooler, reached inside and

selected a diet cola. They carried their selections to the register, setting them side by side on the counter. Chloe started to open her purse, but Donovan already had his money in hand. "I've got them."

She looked as though she wanted to argue, but his expression must have let her know there would be no point. The purchases paid for, he handed her the diet cola and motioned toward the door.

A cloud passed in front of the sun just as they stepped outside, plunging the parking lot into even deeper shadow and making the brisk breeze that skipped around them feel suddenly colder. Once again, Donovan found himself moving closer to Chloe's side.

Chloe looked at him curiously. "Is something wrong?"

He was being foolish, of course. This wasn't one of the rare operations during which he had to flinch at every sound, search every shadow, or suspect every bystander of being armed and dangerous. All he was doing was escorting Bryan's girlfriend for a few hours. Not an assignment he would have chosen for himself, but certainly not a hazardous duty.

Chloe found herself sneaking glances at Donovan again during the remainder of the quiet ride. She regretted that he had slipped on a pair of dark sunglasses when they'd left the convenience store. His face had been difficult enough to read when she could see his eyes, as little as they revealed. Now, all she could see was the hard line of his jaw—which wasn't encouraging conversation.

He would probably be perfectly happy if they completed the rest of the trip in silence. Even when he'd tried to make small talk, he hadn't been particularly friendly. Maybe she shouldn't take it personally. Maybe he was this way with everyone, although she found it hard to believe that charming, congenial Bryan Falcon's closest friend had the personality of granite.

She couldn't say this trip was starting out promisingly. But, at least, she had never had any trouble talking to Bryan, she reminded herself. Just the opposite, in fact; they'd chatted almost like old friends from the first time they'd met.

If Bryan felt more like a good friend than a potential lover—well, that was something she was hoping to overcome during the next few days. Bryan was handsome, personable, intelligent, amusing, attentive—everything a woman could want. She was quite sure that once they were alone, away from the pressure of public scrutiny, their relationship would progress naturally.

She wasn't looking for blazing passion in a marriage, she reminded herself. She wasn't expecting to fall desperately in love—nor to be blindly adored in return. She'd sought those romantic myths before, only to be repeatedly disappointed. She would be content now with security, respect, affection and, most of all, children—and Bryan had almost convinced her he wanted exactly the same things.

Why couldn't Grace understand how appealing his offer sounded?

As for Donovan—Chloe risked a glance at the stern-faced man behind the wheel. He'd made his disapproval clear enough. Did he really think of her as a scheming gold digger, or was he, like Grace, completely turned off by the businesslike way Bryan and

Chloe were going about this courtship? She doubted that Donovan harbored any romantic illusions about love and marriage. She would bet he was convinced she was only after Bryan's money, that Bryan was the one being used.

Well, that was Donovan's problem. She wouldn't waste her breath trying to explain her motives to him. For one thing, it was none of his business. For another, he would never believe her anyway, not if he already had his mind made up about her.

"How much farther is it to Bryan's vacation house?" she asked.

"About another hour."

She nodded and adjusted her seat belt, mentally preparing for another awkward hour. "Will Bryan be waiting for us there?"

"He hoped to arrive about the same time we do—maybe an hour or so afterward if he got held up in New York."

"And will you be staying with us?"

Even though she couldn't see his eyes through his dark glasses, she felt the dry humor in the glance he shot her way. "Don't worry, I won't interfere with your plans. I'll be on my way as soon as you and Bryan are settled in."

She didn't know why his words embarrassed her. There was nothing overtly suggestive about them. But still she found herself averting her face to hide her expression, gazing fixedly out the passenger-side window.

She was an adult, she reminded herself—closing in fast on her thirtieth birthday. She didn't owe Donovan, Grace or anyone else explanations or justifications for her actions. She didn't have to tell them that

Bryan had promised not to rush her, that they had agreed they would spend the next few days talking in private about what they both wanted for their futures.

She'd tried to convince Grace that this was the primary purpose for this intimate retreat, but Grace hadn't accepted it. She was convinced that Bryan was going to pressure Chloe into sleeping with him for a few days. Then, when he grew bored with her, he was going to announce that he'd changed his mind about marriage, leaving Chloe feeling used, betrayed and deeply disappointed.

Chloe suspected that Donovan harbored similar unflattering suspicions about *her*.

She was relieved when Donovan turned off the main highway onto a winding lane that he said led to Bryan's Table Rock Lake vacation home. The sooner this uncomfortable journey was over, the better, as far as she was concerned. She much preferred Bryan's easy charm to Donovan's brooding disapproval.

He made several more winding turns, seemingly taking them miles from anywhere. It occurred to her suddenly that she was being awfully trusting, going blindly into the wilderness with this taciturn man she hadn't met before today. But Bryan had told her she would be safe with Donovan, and she trusted Bryan implicitly. She wouldn't have agreed to spend the next week with him if she didn't.

She had expected Bryan's vacation house to be nice. She already knew he wasn't the type to settle for less.

She hadn't expected anything quite like this.

Looking more like a lodge than a private vacation home, the sprawling structure was built of rock and redwood. Big windows and roomy decks allowed for the enjoyment of the beautiful surroundings—the thick woods, the rolling hills, the glistening lake that lay in the distance behind the house, which perched at the top of a tall bluff. Though tasteful and inviting, there was no question that this place belonged to someone with a great deal of money.

Chloe's family had never been poor, but they would definitely have been categorized as "working class." She'd never been to a place like this that wasn't a public resort.

"Looks like we've arrived before Bryan," Donovan commented, parking in front of the house. "He should be here soon. I'll help you get settled in."

Now that she was actually here, Chloe was unexpectedly hesitant about going inside. Maybe it was because the house was so much more impressive than she had expected, emphasizing the differences between her lifestyle and Bryan's. Or maybe it was a result of the uncomfortable hours she had just spent with Bryan's associate. Or maybe it was because the full magnitude of what she was doing was just hitting her.

This wasn't dinner and a movie, or a night at the symphony—the type of outing she'd shared with Bryan until now. This was a full week with him. Days…and nights. That was enough to daunt her, since going away with a man wasn't something she had done very often. But she couldn't even mark this off as an impulsive fling; the primary purpose of the next few days was to discuss the future. Marriage. The rest of her life.

All the lectures Grace had given her during the past ten days or so suddenly replayed in her mind. Ironically, it wasn't Grace's gloomy warnings that Bryan wasn't serious about marriage that made Chloe so nervous; it was her own deep certainty that he *was* serious.

"Something wrong?" Donovan asked, breaking into her somber introspection and making her realize how long she must have been sitting there without moving.

She swallowed. "No. Nothing's wrong."

Except that she abruptly wanted to go home. Now. As much as she wanted children, as often as she had told herself that there were more sensible reasons to marry than the passionate love of fantasy and fiction, she suddenly found herself suddenly longing with all her heart for the fairy tale. She wanted it *all*—why was she even contemplating settling for less?

Donovan seemed to be studying her intently through his dark glasses. "Changing your mind?"

She lifted her chin and reached for the door handle, determined that he wouldn't see her irrational panic. "Of course not. I was just…admiring the view."

He made a sound that might have expressed skepticism, but she didn't bother to try to convince him further. Before she could change her mind, she opened her door and stepped out of the car.

She hadn't committed to Bryan yet, she reminded herself. He had promised not to pressure her, and she trusted him to keep his word. And who knew? Maybe she *would* fall in love during the next few days. Stranger things had happened.

She wasn't doing a very good job of hiding her reactions to Bryan's Ozarks vacation home. Donovan was aware of the irony in his observation that the woman he suspected of trying to dupe his friend into a marriage-for-money didn't appear to be a particularly skilled actor.

Carrying her bags inside, he watched her face as she took in the professionally contracted decor. Her expressions ranged from impressed to slightly intimidated as they passed through the glass-walled great room, up a curving flight of stairs and down a long hallway to the bedroom suite Bryan had selected for her use.

The luxurious guest suite was located at the farthest end of the hall from Bryan's master suite. Bryan had told Donovan that he and Chloe planned to spend most of this secluded week-long retreat engaging in serious discussions about the future. But Donovan doubted that Bryan intended Chloe to remain at the far end of the hallway throughout the entire week.

"Is, um, something wrong?"

Chloe's hesitant question made Donovan realize that he'd frozen in the doorway of the guest suite, his eyebrows lowered into a heavy scowl. He made a deliberate effort to smooth his expression. He didn't know why he'd been frowning, anyway.

"Just wanted to make sure this room's okay with you before I set your bags down," he bluffed.

Standing in the center of the sitting area that led into the large bedroom, Chloe glanced around at the painstakingly selected antiques and accessories and the invitingly comfortable-looking furnishings. "This looks fine. Perfect."

Maybe it was only nerves that made her sound less than enthusiastic. Maybe just the awkwardness of standing in a bedroom with a near-stranger. Maybe it was that same awkwardness that had his own stomach suddenly tied into knots. "I'll just set these bags beside the, uh, bed,'' he said, then cursed himself for the uncharacteristic verbal fumble.

Chloe nodded and tightened her grip on the bulging tote bag she was holding, as if she were afraid he might try to take it from her.

This was stupid, he thought irritably as he deposited her luggage. While he'd never possessed Bryan's silver-tongued charisma with the ladies, he wasn't usually reduced to stammering. This whole situation was awkward and weird—which must account for the sense of impending catastrophe he'd been fighting ever since they'd stopped at the convenience store.

Leaving Chloe to settle in, Donovan went downstairs to the kitchen. At home there, he opened the refrigerator door and pulled out a soft drink. Popping the top, he downed a third of it in one long guzzle. For some reason, his throat suddenly felt parched.

He would be glad when Bryan arrived so he could get the heck out of this kooky courtship.

As if in response to his fervent wish, the telephone rang. Out of habit, Donovan scooped up the kitchen extension before it could ring a second time. ''Donovan Chance,'' he said automatically—the only way he ever answered a call.

The caller spoke without bothering to identify himself. ''I wasn't sure you'd be there yet. I tried your cell phone. Did you forget to turn it on?''

Donovan reached automatically for his belt. ''Forgot to bring it in. I left it in the car.''

''You didn't have any problems getting there, I hope? The weather's good?''

It wasn't like Bryan to stall with small talk. ''Where are you, Bryan? How long will it take you to get here?''

The sound of a throat being cleared was the only answer, making Donovan's frown deepen. "Bryan? What's going on?"

"Something's come up, D.C. I'm not going to make it there today."

"Damn it, you haven't even left New York, have you?"

"No. The deal here started unraveling this morning and I've had my hands full trying to keep everything together. This is the first chance I've had to even give you a call. I kept hoping I could slip away late this afternoon, but noon tomorrow's going to be the earliest I can get out. I hope to be there by early tomorrow evening."

"And what am I supposed to do with your houseguest in the meantime? Leave her here by herself?"

"I don't think that's a good idea, do you?"

Donovan sighed. "Damn it, Bryan."

"Look, I know you have things you'd rather be doing…"

"Things I *need* to be doing. Like work. Isn't there any way you can hop on a plane tonight and I could take care of things there?"

"I'm afraid not. Trust me, Donovan, this isn't my choice. I'd much rather be there making plans with Chloe than fighting it out here with Childers. I feel like a heel for bailing out on her like this after she's made that long trip. I hope she won't be too angry with me."

"I'm sure she'll get over it," Donovan muttered. Bryan had a way of charming women into forgiving him. Who was he kidding? Bryan's magic even worked on Donovan. He should be steamed over being stuck here like this, but instead, he was agreeing to extend his babysitting services for another twenty-four hours or so.

"So what do you think of Chloe? Is she everything I told you she was?"

"Yeah. She's nice."

The bland words seemed to echo through the phone lines for several long moments before Bryan spoke again. "You have a problem with Chloe?"

"Of course not."

"Something's bugging you, I can tell. What is it?"

"Nothing. I'm just wondering how I'm supposed to entertain her until you get here. She didn't agree to come away on a cozy vacation with me, you know."

"Just keep her company. Take her for a walk or a boat ride or something. Make dinner—maybe throw a couple of steaks on the grill. There's a good selection of DVD movies in the media room, and some new books in the library. Or there's always Scrabble or Monopoly if you get desperate, though I know you're not much of a game player."

With another heavy sigh, Donovan nodded. "We'll get by somehow."

"I'm sure you will. Despite your own glaring personality shortcomings, you'll find Chloe's great company. Maybe she was a bit nervous during the car ride—let's face it, pal, you've been known to intimidate tougher souls than Chloe—but once she's comfortable with you, you'll see how interesting and amusing she can be. Just keep in mind that she's already taken."

"You don't have to worry about that." Donovan hadn't forgotten for one moment that Chloe planned to marry his boss.

"I guess I'd better break it to Chloe that I won't be there tonight."

"She's in her room, unpacking. I'll get her for you."

"Thanks, D.C. I owe you for this."

"You sure do," Donovan muttered, setting the receiver on the counter. "Big time."

She really should have listened to her sister.

Wearing a green satin nightgown and a matching robe, Chloe stood outside on the balcony of the dauntingly elegant guest room. It was a beautiful night—clear, mild, gilded by a bright, nearly full moon—but chilly. Her breath hung in front of her as she leaned against the railing and gazed somberly at the landscape of mysteriously shadowed hills and the glittering lake in the distance. It was a night made for romance and intrigue.

Yet she was spending it alone, wishing she was back in her simple Little Rock apartment.

Grace had warned her that this was a bad idea. She had predicted from the beginning that it wouldn't work out the way Chloe hoped. Little could she have known just how right she would be.

From the moment Bryan had gracefully and effusively apologized for standing her up this evening, Chloe had sensed the plans she'd made disintegrating around her. Or maybe it had all started crumbling even before that—maybe when she'd walked into her living room and found Donovan Chance and her sister glaring at each other.

She wanted to believe she would feel differently now if Bryan had been available to pick her up at her apartment and drive her here himself. If he had been the one to spend the day with her, to dine with her, to bid her goodnight. Instead, she found herself trying to summon a clear mental picture of him. For some strange reason, his image kept metamorphosing in her mind—his thick, glossy black hair and brilliant blue eyes changing to rebellious chestnut-brown strands and metallic-green eyes.

It was obvious that she kept thinking of Donovan because she'd spent so much time with him today. It certainly wasn't anything more than that; she couldn't even say that she liked the man very much. It had been all she could do to make conversation with him during dinner, since he still showed that irritating tendency to answer with a monosyllable any time he could.

The main problem was that at this point, she couldn't say that she particularly wanted to be with Bryan, either, no matter how much more articulate and entertaining he could be than his friend.

She sighed.

"Dreaming of anyone in particular?" a gravelly voice drawled from somewhere beneath her, making her start.

Her heart pounding, she peered tentatively over the balcony. "Donovan?"

On the ground below her, a figure stepped out of the shadows of a bushy tree and into the range of a motion-triggered security light. The resulting yellowish illumination exaggerated the angles and planes of Donovan's firmly carved face, making him appear even more a stranger than he had before. He'd changed from his conservative clothing into a black pullover and black jeans, and he looked very much at home in the darkness.

"What are you doing down there?" She hadn't even realized he was outside, having assumed he was asleep in one of the other bedrooms.

"Just patrolling the grounds."

"So security guard is also on your job description?"

She wasn't surprised when he responded with one of his laconic shrugs, then changed the subject. "Couldn't sleep?"

Leaning her arms against the railing, she looked down at him. "I guess I wasn't as tired as I thought I was."

After a slight pause, he asked, "Want to come outside for a walk?"

"Thanks, but entertaining me *isn't* on your job description."

"Actually, it is. I promised Bryan I'd make sure you aren't bored until he gets here."

Because he made her sound like a cranky toddler he was endeavoring to humor, she replied a bit coolly. "I'm not at all bored."

Bryan had commented often on his second-in-command's commitment; when Donovan Chance took on an assignment, he gave it his full attention. Apparently, he considered her his latest assignment. He was grimly determined to keep her entertained until he could hand her over to his employer. A depressing thought, she discovered, though she didn't care to analyze why.

"I believe I'll turn in now," she said, taking a step back from the rail. "I'll see you in the morning."

He nodded. "Call out if you need anything."

"I'm sure I'll be fine." She couldn't imagine any

reason she would be calling for Donovan Chance during the night.

A shiver went through her as she reentered her bedroom and locked the balcony door. It felt strangely like a premonition—which only reinforced her belief that she was stressed-out about being here at all.

She really should have listened to her sister.

Chapter Three

Donovan didn't require much sleep, but he managed even less than usual during that night. He kept being awakened by the nagging feeling that something was wrong. Or that there was something he should be doing. Because his instincts were so often right, he'd tested all the locks—twice—and he'd patrolled the grounds. He could find nothing wrong, nothing pressing he needed to attend to before morning.

He had to assume he was simply overreacting to the unusual situation he found himself in that evening.

He would be glad when Bryan arrived and he could turn Chloe Pennington over to him—or at least, he *should* be glad. After spending several hours with Chloe, he could understand what had attracted Bryan to her. Had she not already been claimed by his best friend, Donovan might have considered making a move on her, but since Bryan was involved, that, of course, was a line he would never cross.

As for this marriage plan...he still couldn't approve. While he wasn't quite as certain now that Chloe was only after Bryan's money, he still doubted that she had any deep feelings for his friend. There had been some warmth in her voice when she'd talked about Bryan during dinner, but it was almost as if she'd been speaking of a distant acquaintance that she rather liked, rather than someone who should be far more important to her.

He didn't know what her motives were, exactly— whether they were money, security or social connections—but he would bet Chloe wasn't planning to marry Bryan for love. And while Bryan might insist that he wasn't looking for that sort of bond—just as Donovan wasn't interested in falling under some romantic spell—it still seemed that there should be something more to a marriage than amiable companionship.

Shifting restlessly in the bed he usually occupied during his frequent stays here, Donovan told himself he really should mind his own business when it came to Bryan's matrimonial plans. What did he know about marriage, anyway? His own parents had probably considered themselves in love when they married, and that had been a disaster. Bryan's parents could hardly stand each other, but they were still together, apparently content with the arrangement they'd come to during the past forty years.

If Bryan wanted the same sort of cool, convenient alliance, who was he to interfere, even if Bryan would allow him to do so?

Donovan rolled over again in the bed, telling himself to go to sleep and stop fretting about things that were beyond his control. And then he found himself remembering the sight of Chloe standing on that balcony in the moonlight, wearing her floaty nightclothes and looking pretty enough to make a man almost forget how to think.

Donovan was not in a good mood.

Chloe didn't know if he hadn't gotten enough sleep or if he was just bored, but he'd been all but snarling at her ever since she'd joined him in the kitchen. She'd risen early, but he'd already had coffee made and breakfast cooked.

"I hope you like oatmeal," he'd said. "It's one of the few things I know how to cook."

"I like oatmeal," she had answered, warily eyeing his stern expression.

"Good."

She didn't think he'd said a complete sentence since, she mused as they stacked their bowls and spoons in the dishwasher a short time later.

She glanced at the clock on the wall. It wasn't even 9:00 a.m. yet. "What time did Bryan say he would be here?"

If anything, the question only seemed to make Donovan grumpier. "He didn't know, exactly. Late afternoon—early evening, maybe."

The hours in between stretched ahead of her like a gaping hole she had no idea how to fill. She'd packed a couple of books, but it seemed rather rude to close herself in her room for the rest of the day. Or maybe Donovan would prefer that she do just that, freeing him from the responsibility of entertaining her.

After closing the dishwasher door, he ran a hand

through his hair. "It's a nice day out, even though it's cloudy," he said abruptly. "Why don't I show you around the place? You'll probably be spending a lot of time here. It's Bryan's favorite retreat when he needs to get away from the everyday grind."

He seemed to be again assuming that she and Bryan would be married, despite her reminders that she hadn't made that decision yet. Since it didn't seem to serve any purpose to continue reminding him, she merely nodded and said, "All right. I'd enjoy a tour."

He glanced at the thin, coral-colored T-shirt she'd donned with khakis. "You'd better grab a jacket. It's still a little cool out."

For some reason, his words evoked an image of being on the balcony last night, her breath forming silvery clouds in front of her, Donovan gazing up at her from the shadows below. She took an involuntary step backward, as if she could physically move away from that oddly unsettling memory. "I'll be right back."

At least a tour of the grounds would give them something to do for a little while, she reasoned as she pulled on a heavy denim shirt in lieu of a jacket. She was probably growing increasingly aware of Donovan because they had been confined to such tight quarters for so many hours—first in his car, and then in this house. Maybe it would help to be outside.

Donovan was waiting by the back door. He wasn't wearing a jacket, apparently thinking his long-sleeved black pullover and black pants would be warm enough. He'd shown a predilection for black clothing since they'd arrived here, she mused as she stepped outside ahead of him.

Studying him through her eyelashes, she decided it was a good thing he hadn't been dressed this way when he'd arrived at her door to pick her up yesterday. Her over-protective twin might have been tempted to throw herself across the doorstep to prevent Chloe from leaving with this stranger.

Donovan Chance looked just a bit dangerous in black.

As he'd warned her, the air was nippy—though not as cold as it had been last night. The grounds around the house were beautifully landscaped, the plantings lush and natural so that little maintenance was required. Rock and hardwood mulch had been used for pathways through the trees and beds, and several inviting seating areas offered choices of breathtaking lake views, peacefully shaded alcoves or sunbathed clearings. Fountains, waterfalls, birdbaths and feeders added more sensory input.

Chloe was so enthralled by the sheer beauty surrounding her that she almost forgot to watch her feet. She might have taken a tumble if Donovan hadn't reached out to catch her arm, bringing her to an abrupt stop. "Drop-off," he said with his usual brevity.

She glanced down to discover that she stood at the top of a series of flagstone steps that had been carved out of a rather steep hill. The steps were set to one side of the rocky bluff that overhung the lake a hundred feet below. "Do these lead down to the lake?"

"Eventually—in a roundabout way. It takes a bit of exertion—especially coming back up—but Bryan and I go down that way fairly often. Want to check it out?"

She looked cautiously over the edge of the bluff.

It was a long way down—and she'd never been particularly fond of heights. "How steep does the path get?"

Donovan shrugged. "Steeper in some places than others. But it's safe. Bryan wouldn't take any risks with his guests' welfare."

She didn't doubt that. If there was one thing she had learned about Bryan, it was that he was a stickler for details. "Then I'd like to go down to the lake."

"Hang on a second." Moving around her, he walked down a couple of steps, then turned to look up at her. "The stones are still damp, so watch your step."

He was always so conscientious about taking care of her. Donovan really took his assignments seriously, she mused as she moved cautiously onto the first step.

She was glad she was wearing sneakers for the extra traction they provided. Whether because of them, or because she was enjoying the scenery so much, or just because Donovan hovered so protectively nearby, she felt perfectly safe during the descent.

The area was filled with wildlife—birds, chipmunks, rabbits, deer. Two playful squirrels chased each other across the path, oblivious to the two-legged trespassers in their playground. Laughing at their antics, and perhaps a bit overconfident in the traction of her sneakers, Chloe nearly stumbled when her foot slipped on the uneven edge of a stone step. Donovan steadied her instantly, displaying impressively swift reflexes.

"Thanks," she said, embarrassed by her clumsiness. "I guess I've lived in town for too long."

He didn't immediately release her, but kept a loose grip on her arm as he guided her down another short flight of steps to the next sloping walkway. "Did you grow up in Little Rock?"

"No, I'm from Searcy, originally. Our parents still live there, though they left two days ago for a ten-day-long Caribbean cruise. Grace and I moved to Little Rock eleven years ago—right out of high school. We worked days and attended night classes at the University of Arkansas at Little Rock until we earned degrees in business. We always wanted to go into business for ourselves, but we had to wait until the time was right. We opened our shop ten months ago."

It was more than he had asked, of course. Maybe in reaction to Donovan's customary terseness, she tended to babble when he made conversational overtures.

"You and your sister have shared an apartment for eleven years?"

She didn't know whether he found it hard to believe that any two people could cohabit for that long, or if anyone could live with her sister for eleven years—Grace had hardly made a positive first impression with Donovan. She quickly set him straight. "Grace and I don't share an apartment. We did for a while when we first moved to Little Rock, but we found our own places several years ago. Grace was there yesterday to, um, see me off."

"To see you off…or to try one last time to talk you out of going?"

She smiled wryly to acknowledge the hit. "Yes, well…"

Moving ahead of her, Donovan stepped over a large boulder in the path and then turned to offer her his hand. "Careful here. It's slippery."

She hesitated only a moment before placing her

hand in his. His fingers closed around hers, providing support as she made her way carefully over the boulder. He did have a competent air about him. She certainly understood how Bryan had come to depend on him so much.

As soon as Chloe reached the foot of the trail, she decided the trip down was worth the effort. A driftwood-littered gravel beach was shaded by trees that leaned out over the water. On one side of the private inlet sat a neat metal boathouse and a covered wooden deck lined with benches.

"Oh, this is nice." She made a slow circle, peering up the face of the bluff. The back of the house above them was just visible from where she stood. The sun glinted off the many big windows that overlooked the lake. She turned again to study the boathouse and dock. "I suppose Bryan keeps a boat here."

"Two—a ski boat and a pontoon boat. Would you like to go for a ride?"

"Not now, thank you."

"Saving yourself for Bryan?"

The apparent double entendre made her turn to look at him in surprise. Had that actually been a lame joke? If so, it was the first time she'd heard Donovan even attempt to be amusing. Now, how was she supposed to respond? Had she been with Bryan, she would have shot back some similar wisecrack, but with Donovan, her usual wit seemed to get tangled around her tongue.

He didn't wait for her to come up with something to say. Instead, he turned, reached down to scoop up a pebble, and sent it skipping frenetically over the surface of the water.

"Very impressive." She feigned applause. "I

could never do that. Grace, now, is a champion rock skipper.''

He looked skeptical. "You can't skip a rock?"

"Nope," she replied cheerfully. "I've tried since I was seven, and I've never managed more than a sorry bounce or two before my rock sank straight to the bottom. My dad was convinced I just wasn't trying, but I really did try—until I finally gave up in sheer frustration."

"Everyone can skip a rock."

"I can't," she said with a shrug. "Just never figured out the trajectories or whatever."

"*Everyone* can skip a rock," he repeated, looking down at the ground.

"Not everyone."

He bent to pluck several stones from the ground, then rattled them in his palm as he straightened. "Here. Give it a try."

"I'm telling you, Donovan, it's a lost cause. I cannot skip rocks."

"Of course you can." He placed a flat stone in her hand. "Now, just skim it over the water's surface."

"Easier said than done," she muttered, then obligingly tossed the rock at the water. As she'd expected, it sank with a splash.

"No, you threw it into the water, not across it." Donovan handed her another stone. "Think of the water as a solid surface and let the rock hit it at a glancing angle."

"Oh, sure. No problem." She sighed and threw the second rock, watching in resignation when it immediately disappeared beneath the surface. "Okay. Have I convinced you yet?"

"You're not trying."

"If only you knew how many times I've heard that—in exactly that same tone."

He gave her another stone. "Try again. And remember, your object is to skip the rock, not sink it."

That rock made a half-hearted attempt to bounce before it was devoured by a hungry ripple. Chloe turned with a disgusted shake of her head. "I told you. I can't—"

He folded her fingers around another rock. "Try again."

She frowned a little. She didn't quite like the grimly determined look on Donovan's face. He had decided, for some reason, to teach her how to skip a rock—and he didn't seem inclined to give up until she had learned to do so. Because she had a sudden mental picture of herself standing there throwing rocks until sundown, she shook her head. "I'd really rather not. I just can't—"

Her words stumbled to a halt when he moved behind her and covered her hand with his own.

"Like this," he said, pulling her arm back and tilting her hand to a position that satisfied him. "Bring your arm forward and release the rock exactly at that angle."

She had to clear her throat before she could speak. "You're not going to give up until I learn this, are you?"

His low voice rumbled unnervingly close to her ear. "It's just a matter of convincing you that you want it."

"It's, um, not that important a skill to learn."

Without releasing her, he shrugged. "I don't like hearing anyone say, 'I can't.'"

There had to be some significance to that statement,

she mused, trying to distract herself from how closely he stood to her. Something in his past or his psyche made him doggedly stick to a task until it was completed to his satisfaction.

The distraction technique wasn't helping much. She was entirely too aware of the warmth that seemed to radiate from him, and the strength of the hand that held hers. She was definitely spending too much time alone with this man.

She tossed the rock quickly, hoping it would skip so he would move away. It sort of bounced once before sinking.

Sighing, she turned her head to look at him, intending to tell him to forget it. To mark this project off as a lost cause. She couldn't skip rocks, didn't even want to skip rocks, and she saw no reason to waste any more time trying. She was simply going to politely, but firmly, tell him....

Her gaze locked with his cool green eyes...and whatever she had intended to say fled from her mind. His arm was still partially around her, and he stood so close she could feel his breath on her cheek. A quiver of reaction rippled somewhere deep inside her.

It was no longer possible to deny a fact she'd been trying to ignore since she'd first met Donovan Chance. She was very strongly attracted to him. She still couldn't say she liked him—but she was physically drawn to him in a way that worried her.

Though she had tried to tell herself the attraction was simply circumstantial, the rationalization just didn't ring true anymore. She certainly didn't fall for every interesting man with whom she spent time. Which made it even more perplexing that, for the second time in a short period, she found himself intrigued by a strange man.

She moistened her suddenly dry mouth. "Um…"

So abruptly she nearly stumbled, Donovan released her and backed away, shoving his hands into his pants pockets. "Maybe Bryan's the one who should help you with this," he said.

It demonstrated exactly how far her thoughts had wandered when she gaped at him and asked, "What do you mean?"

His left eyebrow lifted fractionally, "Bryan's better at teaching things than I am. He explains things more clearly. He could probably show you how to skip a rock halfway across the lake."

She managed a weak, decidedly fake smile. "I doubt that."

Motioning toward the path they had come down, he moved another step backward. "Ready to head back up to the house?"

"Sure. Bryan could be trying to call us."

His face could have been carved from the same hard rock that made up the bluff behind him. "I have my cell phone. He'd call that number if he wanted to reach us."

Nodding, she made a sign for him to proceed her. "I'll follow you."

"It would probably be better if you go first. Just in case you slip or anything."

She stepped onto the path, but asked over her shoulder, "Still playing bodyguard?"

"I told you. I'm not a bodyguard."

The word always seemed to annoy him. Something else from his past, perhaps. Another little psychological quirk she would probably never understand because she didn't expect to get to know him that well.

She started up the path with as much speed as she could safely manage. She had no intention of falling into his arms, or making a fool of herself in some other way with him.

It seemed the best thing for her to do when she reached the top was to lock herself in her room with a book—rude or not—and try to put Donovan Chance out of her mind. While she was in there, it wouldn't hurt her to do some thinking about her true feelings for Bryan. After all, she'd come here to consider marrying him—only to find herself inordinately fascinated by his best friend.

Definitely something wrong with that picture. Something she should consider very seriously before she made any commitments—to anyone.

It was beginning to look more and more as if Grace had been right all along, she thought somberly, and then winced at the thought of her twin saying, "I told you so."

Donovan hesitated outside Chloe's bedroom door, his hand half raised to knock. For some reason, he was having a little trouble following through with that motion.

After making her way up the path with a speed that had left him almost breathless, she'd closed herself in her room for the remainder of the morning. She'd murmured something about having brought some paperwork along. Rather unexpected, considering this was supposed to be a romantic getaway for her and Bryan—but then, it wouldn't surprise him at all if

Bryan brought a briefcase full of paperwork with him. Maybe Chloe and Bryan really were two of a kind.

Scowling, Donovan rapped on the door more sharply than he had intended.

Chloe opened it quickly. "What is it?"

"It's nearly one o'clock. I thought you might be hungry."

She looked surprised, as if the morning had slipped away from her. "I didn't realize it was so late. I hope you've already eaten."

"No."

"Then you must be starving. Since you cooked breakfast, I'll fix something for lunch."

"Too late. I've already prepared lunch. I hope grilled chicken and vegetables sound good to you."

"That sounds fine, but you really shouldn't have gone to so much trouble. I let the time get away, but I certainly don't expect you to cook for me."

He shrugged. "I had to eat, anyway. I'll meet you in the kitchen when you're ready."

"I'll wash my hands and be right down."

He really hadn't minded preparing lunch; it had given him something to do other than think about Chloe. He had the table set and the food ready to serve when she joined him.

"This looks delicious," she said, taking her seat. "Don't even think about doing dishes after we've eaten. Cleaning up is the least I can do."

He wouldn't argue with her. If doing dishes made her feel like she was pulling her weight, then he wouldn't try to stop her.

"You're a very good cook," she said a few minutes later.

"I get by as long as I've got a grill and a micro-wave."

Glancing toward the state-of-the-art, chef's dream kitchen attached to the sunny nook in which they were eating, she replied, "You have a lot more than that here."

Following her glance, he nodded. "Bryan always goes top-of-the-line."

"Does Bryan like to cook?"

"He knows how, of course. Even though he's al-ways been able to pay for services, he believes every-one should know ordinary living skills like cooking, doing laundry and basic home and car maintenance."

"That's a very practical point of view. If he ever loses his fortune, at least he'll be able to take care of himself."

Donovan knew she was joking. He knew she doubted—as did he—that Bryan Falcon would ever have to count his pennies.

Donovan had no doubt that *he* would still be there if Bryan lost everything. His loyalty to Bryan had nothing to do with fortune or social position. He wasn't confident that Chloe could say the same. If her relationship with Bryan wasn't based on love but on the promise of financial security, then bankruptcy would certainly put an end to that connection.

When he failed to respond to her quip, Chloe changed the subject. "You told me a little about your recent trip to Venice. Has your work with Bryan in-volved a lot of travel?"

"At times."

"Do you enjoy it?"

"My work or the travel?"

"Either."

"I like the work. I tolerate the travel because it's part of the job."

She looked vaguely dismayed, reminding him that she'd told him she dreamed of travel.

"I didn't say I dislike the travel," he said, feeling almost as if should apologize for disappointing her. "I enjoy it sometimes."

He must not have convinced her. She changed the subject again. "Have you worked with Bryan since you finished college?"

He stabbed his fork into a cauliflower floret. "I never went to college, actually. I went into the army after high school."

"I didn't realize that. Bryan said you'd been with him since the beginning."

"We've been friends for a long time. Stayed in touch while he went off to college and I went into the military. When he broke away from his father's company a few years ago to start Bryan Falcon Enterprises, he brought me on board."

"Were you still in the army then?"

"No. I'd been out for a while."

"What did you do in the interim?"

"This and that." He didn't want to talk about those years in between.

He knew she was only trying to keep the conversation flowing, trying to avoid those awkward lapses between them. Lapses during which they both became self-conscious and tongue-tied, when stray glances tended to lock and hold for long moments—until Chloe looked away, her cheeks turning pink and her voice becoming a little breathless. He didn't try to convince himself that she was fighting the same inappropriate attraction he was, but there was definitely an awareness between them.

They'd spent entirely too many hours alone together. It would be better for everyone involved if Bryan arrived soon.

Leaving Chloe to clean up, as she had insisted, he went into the smaller of the two offices in the house, the one he always used here. He turned on his computer and spent an hour replying to the most urgent of his e-mails, trying to keep himself occupied. When the phone rang, he answered it absently.

"How's it going there?"

Bryan's voice brought Donovan's attention away from the computer monitor. "Tell me you're in transit."

"Problems there? You and Chloe are getting along okay, aren't you?"

"Well enough. But she didn't come here to spend time with me. Right now she's probably wishing she'd stayed home."

"What have you been doing today?"

"I've been working most of the day. Parker in L.A. wants an answer by tomorrow morning. And Hamilton's got a proposal she wants us to look over soon."

"You can take care of those things later. I'd rather you keep Chloe entertained now. I don't like to think of her bored and lonely while I'm stuck here for the rest of the afternoon. I know you can be entertaining company when you make the effort, so give it a try, will you?"

Donovan made certain his exaggerated sigh carried clearly through the phone lines. "I really do have more important things to do than to babysit your girlfriend du jour, you know."

The words had barely left his mouth when he happened to glance toward the open doorway. Chloe stood there holding a steaming mug. Her face was completely expressionless, but Donovan knew she had heard his cranky complaint. The set of her shoulders let him know she hadn't liked it.

He cleared his throat. "Er…"

"Let me guess," Bryan drawled, as eerily perceptive as always, "Chloe just walked in."

"Yeah."

"Put her on the line, will you? And, Donovan—after you pry your foot out of your mouth and apologize, be nice to her, okay?"

"Bryan wants to talk to you," Donovan said, holding the receiver toward Chloe without bothering to respond to his friend.

She nodded coolly. "I brought you some coffee. I just made it."

"Thanks. I'll drink it out on the deck while you talk to Bryan."

After swapping the mug for the phone, Chloe turned away from him. Pointedly.

Wincing, Donovan carried his coffee out of the room. It wasn't easy walking with both his feet in his mouth, he decided wryly.

Chapter Four

Though Chloe wasn't watching him, she knew Donovan had left the room by the time she spoke into the receiver. "Hello, Bryan."

"I'm glad you're still speaking to me."

"I'm sure you couldn't help being detained there."

"No. Believe me, I've done everything I can to resolve this mess in a hurry so I can join you there, but it's taking longer than I expected. I can't tell you how sorry I am."

"Does this mean you won't be here tonight, after all?"

"No. I still believe I can get away in time to be there this evening. It could be very late, but we can start our vacation first thing tomorrow morning."

It seemed oddly apropos that a cloud crossed in front of the sun at that moment, darkening the room for a moment. What might have been a frisson of premonition coursed through her. Maybe because the week had started so badly, she had a sudden feeling that she really should suggest to Bryan that he stay in New York.

She'd always believed that when something kept going wrong, perhaps it wasn't meant to be. Grace had said repeatedly that Chloe was making a mistake coming here this week. And then Bryan had been detained. Now Chloe's reactions to Donovan were getting all jumbled and confused—and he thought of her as a gold digger.

Things were definitely going wrong.

It was only her hesitation to ask Donovan to take her home, her reluctance to look wishy-washy or petulant to him, that kept her from canceling everything with Bryan.

"Chloe—about Donovan," Bryan said, as if he'd sensed the direction her thoughts had taken.

"What about him?"

"Don't take him too personally. He doesn't mean to come across the way he sometimes does."

"You're not going to try to convince me his bark is worse than his bite, are you?"

Bryan laughed softly. "No, I'm not going to try to tell you that. But he doesn't bite very often—and never without provocation."

His words weren't particularly reassuring.

Still, she didn't want to seem ungracious, especially since Donovan had been going out of his way to entertain her. His comment about babysitting Bryan's "girlfriend du jour" still stung, though. She hated the idea that he thought of her that way.

She and Bryan chatted for another few minutes,

and then Bryan said he had to go. "The sooner I get back to work, the sooner I can get away," he added.

Chloe hung up the phone, then glanced toward the open doorway. She wasn't looking forward to rejoining Donovan after the crack he'd made to Bryan. She was sure he'd try to apologize, and then they'd get all awkward and embarrassed. It was a scene she would rather avoid, if possible.

She found Donovan in the kitchen, rinsing out his empty coffee mug. "The coffee was good," he said. "Thanks."

"I was making some for myself, anyway."

He set his mug in the dishwasher, then turned to face her. Braced for the awkward apology she expected, she was surprised when he said, instead, "I'm going into town for a few supplies. Want to come along?"

She would like to get out of the house, actually, but there was still that irritating comment hanging between them. "I'm sure you'd like to spend some time by yourself. I have some more paperwork to keep me busy here while you're gone."

"Actually, I'd like you to come along, if you don't mind. I need to buy some groceries, and it will be easier if you're there to help with the selections."

If this was his idea of an apology—or an olive branch, perhaps—it was a strange one. But then, Donovan was definitely a different sort of man from anyone she'd met before.

She still resented being called Bryan's "girlfriend du jour." And she still suspected that Donovan questioned her motives for getting involved with Bryan—and she didn't like him seeing non-existent dollar signs in her eyes. But he *had* given up two days of his busy life to spend time with her in Bryan's absence. He had cooked for her and had done his best to entertain her, she supposed, even though there were things he would admittedly rather be doing. The least she could do was try to be gracious in return, especially since he'd placed her in the position of doing him a favor by going with him.

She kept her reply just a bit cool, because she wasn't going to forget that babysitting crack *too* easily. "Then of course I'll come with you. Just let me get my purse."

She felt him watching her as she left the room, so she kept her chin raised to a regal angle, her back very straight. She intended to make it quite clear to him that she was perfectly capable of taking care of herself. She didn't need a "babysitter"—and that certainly wasn't the way she wanted Donovan to think of her.

Donovan was relieved when Chloe agreed to his plan. He'd concluded that it might be easier to control his thoughts about her if they got out of the house. Out in public with other people.

He probably should have apologized about that babysitting remark. He was fully aware that it still rankled with her. But, damn it, he did feel as if he were babysitting—or bodyguarding, which was even worse.

He didn't know what was wrong with him today—since yesterday, actually. Specifically, since he and Chloe had left her apartment. First there was that itchy sense of impending disaster that had been bugging him for no reason. And then there was his growing physical awareness of Chloe.

It wasn't so strange that he would notice her attributes, of course. She was attractive, if not as stunningly beautiful as most of Bryan's women. Donovan was a normal, healthy male. They'd spent several hours close together. He could still almost feel her slender body brushing lightly against his when he'd stupidly attempted to teach her how to skip a rock. It had seemed like a good idea at the time—something she might consider fun—but he'd quickly realized his mistake.

Standing too close to her—watching her wrinkle her nose in self-derision when she repeatedly sank her stones—hearing her chuckle in resignation at her perceived ineptitude…she'd been entirely too appealing then. Had it been just the two of them involved, with Bryan completely out of the mix, he'd have kissed her there by the water. He doubted that he'd have wanted to stop at kissing.

He *was* sure he would have stopped before discussing marriage—no matter how much he might grow to admire her. He was beginning to strongly suspect that, where Chloe Pennington was concerned, Bryan was thinking with the wrong part of his anatomy.

Not that he blamed his friend entirely for that, he mused, eyeing the slight sway of Chloe's softly rounded hips as she left the kitchen with her shoulders defiantly squared.

To his annoyance, the itchy feeling increased at the back of his neck again the moment he slid behind the wheel of his car. In automatic reaction, he scanned the grounds around them. He saw nothing but trees, brush, rocks, a couple of fat squirrels—nothing to cause him the slightest alarm.

He was beginning to believe he needed a vacation. He hadn't actually taken one in several years.

All during the quiet twenty-minute ride to the nearest town, he tried to ignore that sensation, though he stayed vigilant. There wasn't much traffic in the area, but he found himself studying each battered pickup and late-model sedan that passed them.

Shaking his head in self-disgust, he looked ahead. "Are you in the mood for something sweet?"

"I beg your pardon?"

"There's a little diner near here that serves the best pies I've ever eaten. Want to try it out before we head for the grocery store?"

"Sure. It sounds good."

Though he suspected she was agreeing more for his sake than her own, he nodded and turned right at the next light. The diner wasn't crowded since it was mid-afternoon, too late for lunch and too early for dinner. There were only a couple of vehicles in the small gravel parking lot, which was heavily shaded by the building and several large trees. It was warmer now than it had been earlier, yet, as he pulled into a deeply shadowed parking space, he felt a chill go through him.

He wondered if he was losing it.

"Is your neck bothering you?" Chloe asked from across a small table a short while later.

Realizing he'd been squeezing the back of his neck as if he could make that nagging itch go away, Donovan lowered his hand. "Yes," he said, but he saw no need to elaborate.

"I have ibuprofen in my purse, if that would help."

"It wouldn't. But thanks, anyway."

A waitress with angelic blue eyes and a devilishly

dimpled smile approached their table. "Well, hi, Mr. Chance. Haven't seen you around in a while."

He returned her smile with genuine warmth. "Hello, Judy. It's nice to see you."

"You, too. Mr. Falcon's not with you this time?"

"He's flying in later. I'm sure you'll be seeing him in the next few days. He'll be wanting his pie."

Judy chuckled. "Mr. Falcon does love our chocolate-chip pecan pie. I swear he could eat it every day if he had the chance."

"I'm sure you're right." Donovan nodded toward Chloe. "Judy, this is Chloe Pennington."

"I've seen your picture in the paper," Judy said after studying Chloe a moment. "You're Mr. Falcon's fiancée, aren't you?"

"Well, I..."

"I told Mama your hair was brown. That picture we saw wasn't very good and she was sure it was red, but I told her I doubted Mr. Falcon would be getting involved with another redhead after that last one. Mama never could figure out what he saw in that—"

Donovan cleared his throat. He noted that Chloe looked a bit dazed, but he was accustomed to Judy's chattering. It was her mother who made the pies he and Bryan were so fond of. They'd long since decided that the pies were worth the mostly harmless gossip. "I'll have the coconut pie, Judy. Have you decided what you want, Chloe?"

She glanced at a hand-written list posted on a blackboard near the register. "The lemon meringue, please."

"You want coffee with your pie?" Judy asked, switching easily from gossip to business.

They both accepted, and Judy bustled off.

"I guess I should have warned you that Judy knows everybody's business."

Chloe smiled weakly. "Apparently so."

"Don't let her rattle you. She means well."

"She seems nice."

"She is."

Judy returned and slid two enormous slices of pie in front of them. She looked as though she wanted to stay and talk a bit longer, but a telephone call interrupted her, to Donovan's relief.

Donovan tried to think of something to say to Chloe, but since nothing came to him, he turned his attention to his coconut pie with three-inch-high lightly browned meringue—the diner's specialty. He enjoyed the food—but the itch at the back of his neck didn't go away.

The only conversation between them while they ate consisted of Chloe telling him that he'd been right about how good the pies were here. He replied that he'd been sure she would like them, and then they fell into silence again. Donovan was aware that Judy kept giving them questioning looks, as if wondering why they were there together, and why they were being so quiet, but for once the waitress stayed discreetly in the background. He assumed she had realized that he wasn't in the mood for chitchat today.

There were no other customers in the place when he and Chloe paused at the cash register so he could pay the tab. Judy took his money with a hearty invitation for them to come back soon.

"The grocery store is only a couple blocks away," he said, turning to Chloe just inside the exit door. "If there's anything you particularly want, don't hesitate to say so."

"I would like some fresh fruit," she admitted. "And tea—oolong or Ceylon, if possible. Anything but Earl Grey. I've never developed a taste for that blend."

Donovan rarely even noticed the brand of the tea bags he occasionally dunked in water to make iced tea in the summertime—much less the blend of the leaves encased in the bags. "We'll see what's available."

She reached for the door handle. He beat her to it. With one hand at the small of her back, he opened the door and guided her through it, scanning the nearly empty, gray-shadowed parking lot as he did so.

"You're doing it again," Chloe murmured, eyeing him quizzically. "Acting as if you're guarding me from some supposed danger."

He hesitated a moment, then shrugged, knowing it would do no good to deny that he was on alert. He tried to come up with an explanation that would satisfy her—without revealing the extent of his odd paranoia. "You're involved with a wealthy and powerful man. There are inherent risks in that association, not to mention the possible annoyance of the paparazzi."

"Paparazzi?" She laughed. "I hardly think I'd be of any interest to them."

"You might be surprised," he murmured, noting the way her laughter made shallow dimples appear at the corners of her soft mouth.

As if on an impulse, she patted his arm when they stopped beside the passenger door of his car. "I think it's rather sweet that you're taking such good care of me," she said, her tone gravely teasing.

He surprised himself—and undoubtedly her—by chuckling. "Just doing my job, ma'am."

"I'll be sure and tell your boss to put a commendation in your employee file."

"Do that." He opened her door for her, his faint smile fading at her mention of his boss—the man who *should* be teasing with her in this parking lot. As he headed around the back of the car toward the driver's side, an image of her smile stayed in his mind.

Despite his earlier vigilance, the attack caught him completely offguard. Maybe it was because he'd been so close to getting in his car and driving away. Or maybe because he'd finally talked himself into discounting those nagging, apparently groundless premonitions.

He should have known better. His instincts had always been very accurate. They'd only betrayed him once before—and that, too, had led to disaster.

Something cold and sharp punched into the back of his neck. Someone big and solid pushed him against his car, pinning him there so tightly he could hardly breathe.

Donovan wasn't a small man—six feet tall, a hundred and eighty pounds—but whoever was behind him dwarfed him. Even then, he might have had a chance in a fight—he'd been well-trained in hand-to-hand combat—but whatever had been injected into his neck was already taking effect, blurring his vision, making his stomach lurch.

His legs started to shake, no longer supporting his weight. He would have crumpled had he not been pressed against the car.

He heard a vehicle pull up close to his own, and

got a peripheral impression that it was a van. A side
door opened.

"Chloe," he said, but his voice came out only a
gasping croak. *Lock the doors,* he wanted to yell.
Blow the horn, do something to get attention.

Everything went black before he could make his
unresponsive tongue form the words.

"Wake up, Donovan. Oh, please wake up." Chloe
spoke the words softly, but urgently, trying to penetrate the drug-induced stupor he'd been in since
they'd been taken outside the little diner. She was
concerned that he'd been out so long, and by his pal-
lor and his very shallow breathing.

What if the bastards had given him an overdose of
whatever sedative they had used? What if he didn't
wake up at all? She risked speaking a little louder.
"Donovan? Can you hear me?"

He lay on his back on a bare blue mattress, both
his arms stretched above his head. His wrists were
secured by a pair of handcuffs that had been looped
around one vertical bar of a black iron headboard.
Chloe was on her knees beside him. One end of a pair
of cuffs encircled her right wrist, the other end locked
around another of the iron bars. She'd never worn
handcuffs before, and the metal felt cold and heavy
against her skin.

Since she wasn't wearing a watch, and Donovan's
had been taken away, she had no idea how much time
had passed. She only knew that panic was building
steadily inside her with each passing minute.

Hearing a noise from somewhere else in the house,
she spoke again. "Donovan? Please open your eyes."

A sound rumbled low in his chest—a cross, she

decided, between a growl and a groan. Whatever it was, she'd never heard a more welcome noise. It proved that he was alive—and, she hoped, beginning to rouse. She laid her hand on his chest, just above the spot from where the groan had emanated. "Donovan?"

His eyes opened to bloodshot slits, focusing immediately on her. His voice had a ragged edge when he asked, "Where are we?"

It amazed her that he seemed to wake almost fully alert. No apparent confusion or disorientation. "I don't know where we are. They brought us here in a minivan with the back windows covered, so I couldn't see out."

"How long have I been unconscious?"

"I'm not sure, exactly. It seemed like hours. We were on the road in the van for a long time."

She watched him test the cuffs that bound him as he asked, "Smooth roads? Like highways?"

"No, rough. Like gravel. Lots of turns and hills."

He nodded, then gave the room a slow once-over, apparently noting the one small, grimy window, the dirty wooden floor bare of any furniture except the iron bed, the single closed door. He was still pale, and his eyes didn't look quite right to her, but he wasn't giving in to any aftereffects he might still be suffering. He seemed wholly focused on assessing their situation and figuring ways to get them out of it.

Having taken thorough inventory of his circumstances, he turned his attention to her. "They didn't hurt you," he said, and it wasn't a question. She suspected he'd come to that conclusion after his first glance at her. Typically, his first thoughts had been about business.

"No. I'm not hurt."

"How many of them were there?"

She almost shuddered as she replayed the scene in her mind. "Three. Two attacked you, while another ripped the car door out of my hand before I could close it and lock it. It happened so fast—before I even knew what was going on."

"Did anyone see them grab us?"

"I don't think so. We were parked in that deep shadow and the van pulled up right next to your car, blocking the view from the road or the restaurant. And they moved so quickly...."

"Did you have a chance to scream?"

"They told me they would kill you if I screamed. You were unconscious and the big man held a gun to your head. I couldn't risk your life."

His left eyebrow rose. "So you just got in the van?"

"I didn't have any other choice."

"You saw their faces?"

"They made no effort to hide them."

What might have been a frown flashed across his face. After a moment, he ordered, "Tell me everything they said."

"They said very little. The whole operation seemed to have been carefully worked out ahead of time. They didn't discuss anything. I tried to find out who they were and what they wanted from us, but they just told me to shut up. I rode sitting in the back of the van with your head in my lap and a gun pointed at me." She somehow managed to keep her voice steady despite the lingering terror of that ride.

He glanced at her lap, as if visualizing the scene, and then he said, "I think it's fairly obvious why they grabbed us."

"Is it?" she asked dryly.

"C'mon, Chloe, your name and your photograph have been in the society pages linking you to Bryan. The gossips have the two of you all but married. Even Judy at the diner recognized you. And I'm Bryan's best friend and closest business associate. This is a simple kidnapping with ransom as the objective."

He was confirming a theory she'd already developed. She'd been aware that there were drawbacks to being involved with a man as wealthy and powerful as Bryan Falcon, even before Donovan had pointed them out during the past couple of days, but she'd considered gossip the most troublesome. She had honestly never imagined her personal safety was at risk. Now, of course, she realized she'd been naive not to consider it.

Bryan obviously hadn't made the same mistake. After all, he'd sent Donovan to escort her to the lake house because he hadn't wanted her to make the drive alone. "Did you and Bryan suspect something like this would happen?"

"Of course not." Donovan's reply was sharp and instantaneous. He looked irritated that she had asked. "We didn't have a clue. If we had, do you honestly believe I'd have been so careless?"

Hearing the self-recrimination in his voice, she shook her head. "But you weren't careless. You were so alert that I even teased you about acting like a bodyguard."

"Some bodyguard," he muttered, flexing his hands within their bindings.

He blamed himself. Chloe made another effort to reassure him. "It happened so fast. It was all so well-planned and executed. They had us before either of us could react."

She could tell that he found no comfort at all in her words.

Another sound penetrated the closed door—a muffled thud that might have been another door slamming shut. The sound of a car being started and driven away followed.

"Do you think they're leaving us here alone?" Chloe asked, looking toward the closed door, not certain if she would be dismayed or relieved if their kidnappers had abandoned them.

How long would it take to die of dehydration? But if their kidnappers were going to let them die, wouldn't they have just killed them already? They'd been rough and abrupt, but neither she nor Donovan had been injured.

Donovan didn't seem to share her concern about the possibility of being stranded. "We should be so lucky," he muttered.

She swallowed. "What do you think will happen now?"

Even as he answered, she could tell he was busy studying the room again, and considering their options. "They'll probably wait a few hours before contacting anyone, just to make sure our absence is noted and people have started to worry about us. When enough time has passed, they'll get in touch with Bryan, give him the standard threats if he should contact the authorities, and then offer him their deal for our safe return."

"What do you think he'll tell them?"

Donovan's mouth twisted into his odd half-smile—the one that held little, if any, humor. "What he'll say initially should probably not be repeated in mixed company. After that, he'll negotiate."

"Will he contact the authorities?"

After a quick glance at the door, Donovan merely shrugged.

Was he worried that they were being monitored? Watched, perhaps?

Biting her lip, Chloe glanced quickly around the room, searching for any evidence of a microphone or a video camera. She saw nothing, but then she wasn't exactly an expert on covert surveillance. She didn't know why, but she had a feeling Donovan was more experienced with such matters.

He shifted on the mattress, making her aware that her hand still rested on his chest. She knew she should move it, but she was reluctant to do so. There was something reassuring about the warmth that seeped through his black shirt, and the steadiness of his heartbeat against her palm. She was disinclined to break that fragile connection.

Without thinking, she tried to lift her right hand to brush back her hair, which had fallen into her face. The handcuff jerked her to a stop, rattling loudly against the iron bar of the headboard. "Damn," she muttered, letting her shackled hand fall to her side.

Donovan looked at her tumbled hair. "Your hair was up this morning."

"They took all my hairpins. As well as my purse, your watch, everything in your pockets, both our belts and our shoes." She shivered as she remembered the rough, impersonal pat-down she'd been subjected to while the biggest of the three kidnappers had held her arms behind her back. His grip had been so tight it had brought humiliating tears to her eyes.

"They seem to have covered all the bases in that respect."

She eyed the heavy metal links skeptically. "They thought we could actually use hairpins to pick the locks on these cuffs?"

Donovan moved one shoulder in a semi-shrug. "They might have been right."

The comment brought her eyes quickly back to his face. "You could do that?"

"I could damned well try."

"In that case..." She reached beneath the denim shirt to the coral, pocketed T-shirt she wore beneath, fumbled around for a moment, then produced a sturdy metal hairpin, which she held in front of him.

Chapter Five

Donovan's eyebrows rose. "You always keep hairpins hidden inside your shirt?"

"When I'm wearing my hair up, I do. My hair's fine and it tends to crawl out of restraints during the day. I usually stash an extra hairpin or two in case I need them. I had this one tucked into my T-shirt pocket. It had fallen down into the seam, which must have kept the guy who patted me down from feeling it."

He opened his right hand. "Let me have it."

She placed the pin in his palm, then frowned when he hid it in his own hair instead of setting to work with it. "Can you see it?" he asked.

The thick hairpin was completely hidden in his brown hair. "No. But aren't you going to try to escape?"

"I'll give it a try when I think it's safe to do so."

"And when will that be?"

He glanced toward the little window, which was so dirty that the light from outside barely penetrated it. "Later."

Was he waiting for nighttime? How many more hours would that be? It had been about four-thirty when they'd left the diner. She estimated that they'd traveled for more than an hour in the van, and then perhaps another half hour had passed while she'd waited for Donovan to wake up. It would be dark soon, but she wasn't sure how much longer she could sit here, bound at the wrist, waiting in dread for that closed door to creak open. It had to be worse for Donovan, flat on his back with his arms fastened over his head.

"Maybe we should try now, while we're alone in here. Maybe they assume you're still unconscious. Maybe we could get out through the window before they realize we've gotten free."

"And maybe someone would come in while I'm fumbling with the cuffs and take away the only potential tool we have. I didn't say I *could* pick the lock. I only said I would try. Even if I succeed, it could take a while."

She had to acknowledge his point, as well as the need for caution, but she hated the thought of spending hours here. In frustration, she tugged at the cuff that held her, growing suddenly claustrophobic against the confinement. The only result was the noisy ring of steel against iron, and a stab of pain in her abused wrist.

"Chloe—relax."

"Relax?" She stared at his impassive face in disbelief. "How am I supposed to relax under these circumstances?"

"We haven't been harmed. We're being left alone. There's no reason to panic."

"Yet," she muttered grimly.

"Don't let your imagination run away with you. No threats have been made against us. These are just common thugs looking to make some quick money. Criminal types aren't overly bright, and they almost always make stupid mistakes. We'll wait until they make one with us, and then we'll take advantage of it."

"You make it sound so simple. How do you know they *will* make a mistake? How do you know they aren't planning to take the money and then kill us? They let me see their faces." She hated the tremor in her voice, the fear she couldn't hide. Especially since Donovan seemed so unnaturally calm and controlled.

But when she looked into his eyes, she saw that he wasn't as controlled as she had believed. His usually cool green eyes were a dark emerald now, gleaming with an anger so hot she could almost feel the warmth. She'd thought his face was expressionless; now, she saw that the muscles beneath his taut skin were tensed into a steely mask. No, most definitely, he was *not* calm.

"They aren't going to hurt you," he vowed, his voice a low growl.

She sat back on her heels for a moment to study him. Beneath her hand, his heart continued to beat steadily, but the pounding seemed a bit faster now. Stronger. "Tell me what you want me to do," she said simply, literally placing her life in his hands.

"Just stay calm and let me handle things now. I'll keep you safe."

Her gaze still locked with his, she moistened her lips and nodded. "Thank you."

He was the one who looked away first. "Bryan's counting on me to watch out for you," he said gruffly.

She swallowed and took her hand off his chest. "This is more than you signed on for when you agreed to 'babysit' for a few hours, isn't it?"

"As I said—I didn't expect this at all. If I had, I wouldn't have been caught off guard, not even for a moment. As for the babysitting crack—well, don't take that personally."

Studying his uncomfortable position, and the dark circles under his eyes that were so noticeable, she knew she couldn't hold a grudge now. "Don't worry about it," she said. "I'm sure you were frustrated because you were being kept from your work for so long."

"That's one explanation," he muttered.

Before she could ask for clarification, the doorknob turned and the door opened. Instinctively, Chloe moved closer to Donovan—though she couldn't have said whether it was to seek protection or to offer it.

The man who walked in was the smallest of the three who had blindsided them. Dark-haired, dark-eyed, his narrow face half covered with a sparse, patchy beard, he walked with a hunch-shouldered shuffle and spoke with a smoker's raspiness. "Y'all need some water or something?"

"We need the keys to these cuffs," Donovan retorted, rattling his restraints.

Their captor gave him a remonstrative look. "Let's not waste time with irrelevancies."

"I would say letting us go is very relevant to your welfare."

Though it was exactly what she had expected, Chloe wished Donovan wouldn't challenge the other man quite so aggressively. It wasn't as if he could defend himself in his current position. Fortunately— at least in her opinion—the other man didn't allow himself to be baited. He looked instead at Chloe, pointedly ignoring Donovan. "Are you comfortable? Is there anything you need?"

"Comfortable?" She looked at the handcuffs. "Hardly."

"Sorry about the restraints. I'm sure you can understand the need for them."

Donovan made a sound of disgust. The other man flicked him a look and then turned back to Chloe. "I can bring you some water, if you like."

"No." She almost added an automatic thank you, stopping herself just in time. She wasn't about to thank her kidnapper for anything short of letting her go.

He nodded. "Call out if you need anything."

With that, he turned and left the room, closing the door firmly behind him.

Donovan muttered an expletive beneath his breath, bring her attention back to him.

"I'm surprised you didn't ask him any questions," she commented. "Like what they want, how long they plan to keep us, what their next step is."

"Questions weren't necessary," he murmured, his gaze still fixed on the door. "I know exactly what's going on."

She frowned. "You learned something from him just now?"

He nodded.

After a moment, she prodded. "Well?"

"Find that hairpin for me, will you?" he requested, instead of explaining.

"Donovan…"

"Let's save the conversation for later."

Something about his tone gave her a renewed sense of urgency. Biting her lower lip, she ran her left hand through his hair until she found the hairpin he'd hidden. He winced a little when she pulled it out. "I'm sorry. Did I pull your hair?"

"Doesn't matter. Put the pin in my right hand."

She did so, then sat back again while he fumbled with the pin and the cuffs. He dropped the hairpin once, which caused him to curse and her almost to panic until she was able to find the pin on the mattress beneath his hands. They both breathed sighs of relief when she gave it back to him.

"If I could just see what I'm doing," he grumbled, starting again.

"Have you done this before? Picked a lock with a hairpin, I mean."

"Once or twice," he answered distractedly, his concentration focused on what he was doing above his head.

Chloe had a feeling there were some interesting stories behind that reply, but this, of course, wasn't the time to ask. For one thing, she didn't want to distract him, possibly causing him to drop the hairpin again.

She didn't know how much time passed while she sat there watching him, listening to him mutter beneath his breath in frustration. Once they heard something crash in another part of the cabin, and they both froze, their heads whipping in the direction of the door. After a moment, Donovan went back to work on the lock.

It was getting darker outside, and their captor hadn't turned on the overhead light when he'd left them. Long shadows filled the room now. The fierce determination in Donovan's eyes made them seem to gleam like a cat's eyes in the gloom.

The lock opened with a muted click. Such a quiet and anticlimactic sound that Chloe almost didn't realize its import. When she did, she caught her breath. "You got it?"

He freed his left hand, lowering it to his side and flexing it to restore the circulation. His right wrist was still shackled, but he unhooked the cuffs from the headboard and levered himself into a sitting position. He swayed. Chloe reached out with her left hand to steady him. For just a moment, he leaned against her for support.

"The sedative must still be affecting you," she murmured, her free arm around him. "Are you okay?"

"A little nauseous, but it's passing."

Drawing a deep breath, he straightened and reached for her cuffed wrist. "Let me see if I can get this open."

Another distant sound made her heart beat faster. "What are you going to do if he catches you doing this?"

"My hands are free now. I won't be taken without a fight this time."

"He's the one who had the gun earlier. What if he still has it on him?"

Instead of answering, Donovan bent his head closer

to her wrist. Even with his hands free—though the cuff still dangled from his right wrist—and with her in front of him, he couldn't immediately free her. Chloe was beginning to worry that this was taking too long, that the dark man would return and catch them.

She kept picturing him holding that gun to Donovan's head while Donovan had been unconscious and vulnerable. She'd had no doubt then that he would pull the trigger if she refused to cooperate, just as she had little doubt that he would shoot them now if he caught them trying to escape—no matter how solicitous of her welfare he'd pretended to be earlier.

Of the three men who had ambushed them, she'd gotten the impression that the small, dark man hadn't been in charge, but he'd been the most dangerous.

"Maybe you had better go without me," she urged in a whisper, as if their captor had his ear pressed to the other side of the door. "You can bring the police back..."

"I'm not going anywhere without you." Donovan's tone was pure steel, making it clear that he expected no argument.

She might have argued anyway, had the lock not given way at that moment. Relief flooded through her when he removed the cuff from her wrist. She shook her hand vigorously. The bracelet hadn't been overly tight, but just being restrained had made it feel as though it were squeezing her.

"Okay?" Donovan asked.

"Yes. Thank you. What do we do now?"

Donovan slid off the bed, his movements steady now, and reached a hand out to Chloe. "We get the hell out of here."

His fingers closed firmly around Chloe's when she took his hand and climbed as silently as possible off the bed. The bed frame creaked when she moved off it, causing her heart to stop for a moment, but Donovan was already moving toward the window. Their stockinged feet made no sound on the wooden floor.

"Damn it."

Chloe had been looking anxiously over her shoulder toward the door. Donovan's mutter brought her head back around. "What? Is the window locked?"

"Nailed shut. There's no way I'll get it open without being heard."

She bit her lip, swallowed, then asked quietly, "Now what?"

In a seemingly automatic gesture, he reached out to run the knuckles of his left hand along her jaw line. "I'm still going to get you out of here."

The brief but oddly intimate contact caught her off guard, causing her to freeze for a moment. Motioning her to stay where she was, Donovan moved silently across the room to the door. With his left hand resting on the doorknob, he listened through the wood for a moment, then tried the knob. It wasn't locked.

"They weren't expecting us to get free," he murmured.

"So what do we do?" Her voice was barely loud enough to reach her own ears.

Holding up his left hand in a silencing gesture, he opened the door a bit wider and peeked carefully out. The handcuff still dangled from his right wrist, but he tried to keep it quiet.

Holding her breath, Chloe tiptoed a bit closer to him, peering over his shoulder into the short, dark hallway outside the room. A gleam of light at the far

end indicated where their captor waited. She heard
the faint strains of music coming from that direction.
A radio, perhaps?

She imagined him sitting in the main room, reading
and listening, patiently killing time until his cohorts
rejoined him. And then what?

Donovan must have heard something she didn't. He
eased the door closed again and put a hand on her
forearm. "Back to the bed," he murmured. "Get in
the same position you were in before."

"But…"

"Hurry." He almost pushed her back to the bed.
Once she was kneeling there, he handed her the
closed cuff he had removed from her right wrist.
"Hold this at your side," he ordered. "Keep your
arm down, as if you're still wearing the cuff."

He was already stretching into the position he'd
been in earlier, flat on his back, hands above his head,
gripping the empty end of his own cuffs so that it
wasn't immediately apparent that he wasn't restrained.

Chloe heard footsteps coming down the hallway
now. "What do you want me to do?" she whispered,
her heart in her throat.

"Just stay out of my way."

The door opened as the words left Donovan's
mouth. The dark man entered, carrying two small
plastic cups of water in his left hand. He looked distracted, which Chloe hoped was a good sign. "I
brought water," he said. "You'll get something to eat
later, when my partners return."

Chloe didn't want to think about his partners returning just yet.

Donovan glared at him. "I hope you're planning

to unlock these cuffs. I can't drink lying flat on my back.''

''Yeah, nice try, Chance. But don't worry, I won't let you drown.''

The dark man walked closer to the bed, extending one of the cups toward Chloe. Suddenly terrified that he would notice the empty bracelet in her hand, she looked quickly at Donovan.

A muscle flexed in his cheek. It was the only warning of his intentions. A heartbeat later, he made his move, coming off the mattress in one smooth, powerful motion. The dangling handcuff clattered against the iron headboard, and the bed frame squeaked loudly. The two cups of water flew, splashing all of them.

Caught completely off guard, the dark man was engaged in a fight almost before he realized what was happening. He stumbled and went down, hitting the wooden floor with a crack.

The scuffle didn't last long. Using his fists and the heavy handcuff bracelet, Donovan efficiently rendered the other man unconscious. Even though she acknowledged the necessity for it, Chloe was a bit taken aback by the cold, controlled violence of Donovan's actions.

She'd thought once before that he looked dangerous dressed in black. Now she knew that he *was* dangerous—no matter what he wore.

He stood and wiped a trickle of blood from the corner of his mouth with the back of his left hand. Apparently, his opponent had gotten in a few defensive blows. ''You said you saw this man with a gun?''

Chloe took a tentative step forward. ''Yes. He was the only one I saw with one earlier.''

"He doesn't have one on him now. It must be in the other room."

A flash of light through the window made Chloe gasp. "That's a car. The others are coming back."

"We'll go out the back. Come on."

He caught her hand, almost pulling her with him as he moved rapidly toward the door. She didn't take time to look around the shabby cabin as they rushed through it. She just wanted out.

A swinging door at the back of the sparsely furnished main room led to a cramped kitchen. Still half-dragging Chloe behind him, Donovan turned the doorknob, shoved the door open and barreled through it.

The cabin was obviously remote. There were no lights to guide their way across the small clearing that lay behind it. They stumbled several times before plunging into the dense forest that crowded around the clearing.

Trying to force her eyes to adjust to the darkness, Chloe looked up at the sky. Tree limbs just leafing out for summer partially blocked the pale moon from her sight. The faint illumination it provided gave them little assistance in making their way across the rocky, uneven ground. Donovan's black clothes made him blend perfectly into the darkness. She was painfully aware that her light khaki pants, denim shirt and coral T-shirt were all too visible.

Already, her thin socks were torn, and she was sure there was a fairly deep cut on her right foot. Afraid that their captors could be right behind them—with shoes, flashlights and guns—she tried to ignore her discomfort and keep moving forward, but she couldn't help stumbling several times. She might have fallen more than once if Donovan had not provided support.

She couldn't help wondering why it seemed easier for him. Was he more accustomed to walking almost barefoot across rocky ground?

"Do you think they're chasing us?" she asked breathlessly.

He helped her over a fallen log. "They won't just let us go. We have to keep moving."

"Can we—" She winced when her foot fell on a spiny pinecone. "Can we get to the road?"

He didn't slow down as he answered in a low voice, "They'll be patrolling the road. Our best bet now is to get as far away from them as possible. They can't know which direction we've gone, so it won't be easy for them to follow."

"But—"

"Chloe." He put a hand at the small of her back, the gesture both supporting her and urging her forward. "Don't talk. Move."

Biting her lip, she made a grim effort to comply.

It was a nightmarish journey. Rocks, fallen branches, pinecones and other debris stabbed into the soles of her feet. Tree branches slashed at her face. Deep holes and sheer limestone bluffs made their passage even more treacherous.

Staying very close to Donovan, Chloe locked her jaws and pressed onward. She was winded, exhausted and in pain, but she refused to given in to her weaknesses in front of Donovan. She would keep going as long as he did—or die trying.

The latter seemed more likely, she thought, a ragged gasp escaping from her when her ankle twisted excruciatingly on a rough patch of ground. She limped after that, but she didn't stop.

By the time Donovan tugged her to a stop, she had entered a zone—moving without thinking, without feeling, without looking from side to side. Swaying on her feet, she blinked at him, barely able to focus on his deeply shadowed features. She concentrated on his eyes, which reflected the faint glow of the moon as he studied her intently.

"Are you all right?" His voice sounded odd—muffled, hollow, distant.

"I'm fine," she answered automatically, her own voice sounding like a stranger's.

"You have to rest. I think it's safe to do so now."

"I can keep going," she insisted, exerting an effort to lift her chin.

"Then *I* need a rest." Still holding her arm, he looked around for a moment, then nudged her toward a large tree. "We'll sit here for a while."

They settled carefully on the ground beneath the tree. The rock-, leaf- and twig-covered ground didn't make a particularly comfortable seat, but it was such a relief to be off her feet that Chloe didn't even think about complaining. She leaned back against the rough bark of the tree with a weary sigh.

The sigh changed almost immediately to a gasp of pain.

Donovan turned quickly toward her. "What's wrong?"

"My feet," she gasped. Spears of pain stabbed upward from the soles of her feet through her legs, up her back, all the way to the base of her neck. There wasn't an inch of her that didn't hurt, but the pain was especially concentrated in her abused feet.

Donovan scooted around to take her right foot in his hands. He had no light to examine her closely, but he ran his fingertips lightly over the bottoms of her torn and filthy socks. As light as his touch was, she winced when she brushed a deep cut. He set her right foot down very gently, then repeated the motions with her left.

"You're bleeding from several cuts. They probably have dirt, maybe even tiny pieces of gravel embedded in them. You've also got some bad bruises and scrapes. It's no wonder you're hurting."

"Aren't *you?* You aren't wearing shoes, either."

"I have a few cuts, but not as many. The bottoms of my feet are more callused than yours."

Of course they were. Her head back against the tree, Chloe closed her eyes and swallowed a moan. She hated looking so weak in front of this tough, strong and very self-sufficient male, but she had just about reached her limit.

"Anybody ever tell you that you're tougher than you look?" Donovan asked as he set her feet carefully on the ground.

A single tear escaped from her right eye. "There's no need to try to flatter me now."

"I don't flatter. I just state facts." He scooted around until he was sitting beside her again and then he pulled her against his shoulder. "Get some rest," he said gruffly. "We're safe for now."

Safe? They were sitting in an unknown forest in pitch darkness while three armed kidnappers searched for them. They had no lights, no food or water, no way to call for help—not even any shoes. They were hardly safe.

And yet she found herself relaxing against Donovan's side, her breath escaping in a long, tired sigh. Allowing herself to float on waves of pain, she closed her eyes and tried to turn off her thoughts.

She would be strong again later. For now, she simply had to rest.

Chapter Six

Donovan didn't know if Chloe was sleeping or just drifting. Her breathing was deep and even, her body warm and limp against his. Remembering the condition of her feet—at least from what he could tell in the dark—he wouldn't blame her if she were whimpering at this point.

Definitely tougher than she looked.

Sitting very still so he wouldn't disturb her, he took a quick assessment of his own physical condition. His face was a little sore from close contact with the other guy's fist. The heavy, skin-chafing handcuff was still clasped around his right wrist, the closed left bracelet still dangling. He'd lost the hairpin back at the cabin, but the annoying weight around his wrist was the least of his problems at the moment.

Chloe sighed and shifted against him. Suspecting that her discomfort was keeping her from resting well, he wrapped his left arm around her and pulled her more snugly into his shoulder. She murmured something unintelligible and nestled into him, hiding her face in his throat as if to hide from everything that threatened them.

No one was getting to her without going through him first, he vowed. And then he loosened his hold on her a bit as he remembered that it was his job to protect her. For Bryan.

Not that he expected Bryan to appreciate his efforts so far. He'd antagonized Chloe's sister, bored Chloe into closing herself in her room with a stack of paperwork, and then carelessly let them get taken captive. He hadn't been careful enough, hadn't been vigilant enough—even though he'd sensed that something was wrong.

He should have listened to his instincts, kept his guard up. Instead, he'd let himself get distracted by…well, by things he'd had no business noticing.

A strand of Chloe's hair tickled his cheek. Without thinking, he reached up with his right hand to brush it away, nearly conking her with the swinging handcuff bracelet. He caught it just in time, then spent several minutes berating himself for almost causing her more pain.

He'd tried to tell her he was no bodyguard. Not anymore, anyway.

He'd say their present circumstances provided ample proof of that.

It was still dark when Donovan roused Chloe. "We should probably move on," he said.

"How long have we been resting here?" she asked groggily, lifting her head from his shoulder.

"I'm guessing about an hour. I haven't heard any sounds of pursuit, but I know they're looking for us somewhere. We can't just sit here and wait for them to find us."

She drew a deep breath and pushed herself upright. The very thought of standing made her want to groan, but she clenched her teeth and accepted Donovan's hand when he rose and extended it to her. The groan almost escaped when her battered feet immediately protested her weight, but she bit it back and took a few halting practice steps. The pain was intense, but she could handle it because she had no other choice. "Which direction?" she asked.

Donovan ran a hand lightly over her tumbled hair in what seemed like a gesture of approval. "Do you want to hold my arm for support?"

"I'll probably have to do that later," she admitted. "But I'll try to make it on my own for a while."

His nod was just visible in the gloom. "Then let's go."

Maybe she took some small comfort in noticing that Donovan was limping, too. While it was reassuring to believe that Donovan was totally in control of this situation, it was also a little nice to know he wasn't completely immune to the mortal weaknesses that were affecting her.

She forged on, following him deeper into the forest, trusting him to make decisions on her behalf. For now.

She started counting her steps. One, two, three, four…the silent cadence was the only thing that kept her moving forward. She told herself that if she could just take ten more steps…and then ten more…she would survive.

They made it over the rocks and fallen limbs that blocked their way, through the heavy brush that appeared in clusters to tangle their feet, along the edge of the many bluffs that filled the mountainous region. "Do you know where we are?" she asked Donovan at one point. "Do you know how to get to a road or a phone?"

"No," he answered simply. "At this point, I couldn't even say what state we're in, though I assume it's either Missouri or Arkansas."

So they were lost. But at least they weren't handcuffed to an iron bed frame at the mercy of three kidnappers. Ten more steps, she told herself, pressing forward. Ten more steps...and then ten more...

Again, it was Donovan who brought them to a halt beside a small, running stream they could easily step over. He knelt beside it and scooped a handful of water into his mouth.

"It isn't safe to drink water from a stream like that," Chloe pointed out automatically.

"I don't happen to have any purification tablets on me. Do you?"

Because she knew the question was rhetorical, she didn't answer.

"Have a drink," he urged. "Just a small amount. You don't want to dehydrate."

Images of microbes and pollution flitted through her mind, but she was thirsty. Just the sound of the trickling water made her mouth feel dry. She knelt beside him.

The water shimmered black in the moonlight. It felt cold when she dipped her hands into it. The night air was cool against her overheated face. She might have felt cold had they not been exerting themselves so much.

The water tasted just a little metallic, but it felt good as it slid down her throat. An owl hooted above her as she swallowed another handful. She had been only marginally aware of the nightlife that shared the forest with them. The occasional rustling in the leaves, or flutter of wings, or distant cry—she'd heard them all, but hadn't paid much attention. Nor had she worried about any wild animals they might encounter.

The predators that frightened her most tonight walked on two legs, not four.

Donovan helped her back to her feet. "You need to rest again," he said, his hands on her shoulders.

"Is it safe?"

"I think so. We've put a lot of distance behind us, and I've been changing direction frequently. It won't be easy for them to track us."

She hadn't even noticed that he'd changed directions. "Can we hide somewhere to rest?"

She didn't like the thought of dozing out in the open again where anyone could stumble onto them.

"Exactly what I had in mind."

He helped her over the stream, then led her a short distance farther to a bluff that rose straight above them. Surely he wasn't expecting her to climb now.

Instead, he pushed a low-hanging branch out of the way to reveal a darker area on the shadowed face of the bluff. "A cave," he said. "I spotted it when I bent down to drink."

Apparently his night vision was better than hers— which shouldn't surprise her. She eyed the dark hole warily. "What if there's a bear or a mountain lion or a family of snakes in there?"

"I'll check." He bent to pick up a good-sized branch at his feet, then moved forward. "Wait here."

Chewing her lower lip, she watched as he bent to poke cautiously around in the hole. She held her breath when he moved farther into the opening. She didn't like having him out of her sight even for that short time, and she was relieved when he reappeared in front of her.

"It looks clean," he said. "And it's well hidden. We'll be safe in there for a while."

When she hesitated, he flashed her a smile, his teeth gleaming for a moment in the darkness. "Have I led you wrong so far?"

It was the first time she actually remembered seeing him smile—and he'd picked a hell of a time for it, she thought with a shake of her head. And yet it disarmed her enough that she moved with him toward the cave.

Cave was a generous description, she discovered when she ducked into the opening with him. *Hole* was more fitting. Indentation, maybe. There was just enough room for the two of them to sit side by side with their legs stretched in front of them. The back of the cave was a bit damp and slimy. For all she knew it could be covered with creepy-crawlies.

She didn't care. She leaned gratefully back, her body going limp against the rock. Shoulder to shoulder, she and Donovan sat in silence while they let their breathing and heartbeats slow from the strenuous hike.

She couldn't see him at all now. No light penetrated the opening. She was glad their shoulders were touching—just for the reassurance of contact, she told herself, closing her eyes. No other reason, of course.

* * *

When she opened her eyes again, the gray light of a cloudy dawn was filtering into the cave and she was lying curled on her side with her head on Donovan's thigh.

With a slight gasp, she lifted her head.

"It's okay." Donovan sounded completely alert, making her doubt that he'd slept at all. "We're safe."

Had he sat there guarding her all this time? She cleared her throat as she righted herself, pushing a hand through her tangled hair. "I'm sorry. I don't know how I ended up in that position—"

"I put you there." He shifted his weight, indicating that he'd gotten a bit cramped serving as her pillow. "You fell asleep. You looked uncomfortable, so I shifted you a little."

She tried to put the feel of his solid thigh out of her mind. "Did you get any rest?"

He shrugged. "Just sitting still felt good."

Maybe their arduous trek had been more difficult for him than he had allowed her to see.

Now that she had a little light, Chloe decided to risk a look at her feet. Sitting cross-legged, she turned her soles toward her. The sight made her grimace.

The bottoms of her once-white socks were now black with dirt and dried blood, with gaping holes revealing the bruised and shredded skin beneath. She didn't even want to think about removing the socks yet. When that time came, they would have to be peeled away—and that was going to hurt.

Still leaning back against the cave wall, Donovan watched her. "You haven't walked barefoot much, have you?"

"Not much," she admitted. "When I was young,

I stepped on a nail once. It tore into my skin and I had to have a tetanus shot. I was so traumatized by that experience that I refused to go barefoot for years. I never got into the habit. Even at home I always wear slippers.''

"That explains your delicate feet. The walk last night must have been hell for you.''

"It wasn't easy. What about you? Are you in the habit of going barefoot outdoors?''

Again, his shoulders moved in a shrug. "I almost never wore shoes when I was a kid. Typical Arkansas redneck kid—wild and barefoot.''

She found it hard to reconcile the composed and sophisticated man who had arrived at her doorstep—the man who had just returned from Venice, who moved among politicians and captains of industry, Bryan Falcon's best friend and trusted confidant—with his description of a wild, barefoot "redneck kid.''

"So, did you spend much time in the woods?'' she asked lightly.

"A fair bit. Why?''

She placed a hand on her hollow-feeling stomach. "I was sort of hoping you'd know how to scavenge breakfast.''

"I usually carried a bag of supplies with me when I spent a day in the woods.''

She sighed wryly. "Oh, well. I suppose it won't hurt me to diet for a couple of days.''

He gave her a leisurely once-over. "You hardly need to diet.''

She looked quickly toward the cave opening to hide an unexpected and unwelcome blush. "I'm very thirsty again. Maybe I'll risk another drink of that stream water before we move on.''

Donovan's reply was lost in a loud crash of thunder. Chloe started, proving that she was still very much on edge no matter how calm they were both pretending to be. ''It sounds like it's going to rain,'' she said, trying to cover her jumpiness with nonchalance.

The sound of a hard rain filled the cave almost before she'd completed the sentence. A gust of wind pushed a fine mist inside, chilling the cool air even more.

''Yeah, I think it might rain,'' Donovan murmured.

''Great.''

''That's not such a bad thing. Any tracks we might have made last night will be eradicated by a downpour this heavy.''

She knew he was trying to put a positive spin on their circumstances for her sake. She appreciated the effort. ''What's our agenda now?''

''We can wait out the rain here for a while. There's no need to go out in it.''

''And when the rain stops?''

Looping his arms around his upraised knees, he looked toward the opening. ''We move on.''

She kept her own legs outstretched, keeping her poor feet as still as possible. The thought of hiking several more miles was hardly pleasant. The cave was dry and well-hidden—both of which made her reluctant to leave—but they couldn't wait here for rescue. For one thing, no one was looking for them—except their kidnappers.

''Do you think we'll be able to find our way out of the forest before...well, before anyone finds *us*?''

"We're going to be very careful about who finds us. Our biggest problem right now is figuring out which direction to go when we leave the cave. We're probably in the middle of several thousand uninhabited acres. If we go deeper—farther from civilization—it could be days before we stumble across anyone. I hate to risk going that long without food."

"But if we go back the way we came, we could run into the kidnappers."

"Exactly. I'm sure they're still looking for us—and they might well have brought back-up."

"So?"

"We do our best," he replied. "I'll make some educated guesses—and we'll hope for some luck."

"Are you usually lucky?"

It was nothing more than a quip, intended to keep the conversation light. But instead of smiling, Donovan frowned and let the question pass unanswered.

After an awkward moment, Chloe tried again to keep him talking. The weather was always a nice, neutral subject, she figured. "It sounds as though the rain has settled in for a while."

He nodded. "It's coming down hard."

She pulled the denim shirt more snugly around her. "It's getting colder."

"Not much. It's just that the air blowing in is damp, which makes it feel cooler."

"At least the cave is a bit elevated, so the water isn't running in."

She didn't even get a monosyllabic reply that time—just a grunt. They might as well have been back in the car again—only this time she didn't even have passing scenery to entertain her.

It could turn out to be a very long morning, she

thought, leaning back against the cave wall. But at least they were dry, and safe for the moment. She would concentrate on those positive points for now.

She had never been very good at estimating passing time. She'd been sitting close to the cave opening, watching the rain fall in the woods outside, for what seemed like a very long time when she broke the silence to ask, "I wonder what time it is."

Donovan roused from his deep introspection to reply, "Just guessing, I'd say mid-morning. Maybe ten, ten-thirty."

"I hope Grace hasn't heard we're missing yet," she said, vocalizing a concern that had been nagging at her all morning. "She'll be frantic."

"I suppose that depends on whether Bryan chose to contact her—and my prediction is that he won't until he has more information."

"So you think Bryan has been contacted by the kidnappers?"

"Probably. I expect that's what the other two were doing while they were gone."

"You've known Bryan a lot longer than I have. What do you think he's doing now? Has he contacted the police? Called my sister?"

Donovan gave it a moment's thought before he answered. "He hasn't called the police. And he won't take any chance of a media leak, so he probably hasn't told your sister, either."

"So what *is* he doing?"

"He's looking for us. He has contacts. They'll be on our trail quicker than any official agency would be."

"What was it you learned when that man offered

us water yesterday? When he left the room, you said you knew then what was going on.''

Donovan's response caught her by surprise. ''I recognized him.''

Wide-eyed, she scooted around to face him more fully. ''You know him? Who is he?''

''I didn't say I know him. I said I recognized him. I don't think he realized it.''

''So you've seen him before, but you were never introduced?''

''Right. I saw him leaving an office that I was about to enter. It was a couple of weeks ago in New York. The guy probably never saw me—and if he did, he probably doesn't suspect that I recognized him.''

''How *did* you recognize him?''

One of his typical shrugs was followed by, ''I have a good memory for faces.''

''You're sure it was the same man?''

''Yes.''

''So he was in New York. Do you know who he works for—or do you think he and his two cronies cooked this scheme up on their own?''

Donovan shook his head. ''I'd put my money on the CEO of the company Bryan's been trying to take over during the past couple of weeks. It's a hostile takeover, but everything was in place, all the details ironed out. That's why Bryan and I were surprised by the last-minute glitches that cropped up to detain him in New York. They're annoying and time-consuming, but they wouldn't have stopped the takeover.''

''You think Bryan was deliberately detained so we could be taken?''

''Seems too coincidental not to consider that possibility.''

"So you think the condition of our release is for Bryan to stop his takeover attempt?"

"No, nothing that obvious. I'd imagine it's a straightforward demand for ransom. Childers has been complaining that he didn't get enough for his company shares, even though he got all he deserved, probably a bit more than he deserved. Looks like he decided to make a little extra on the side."

"Childers—that's the CEO you mentioned?"

Donovan nodded.

"And he's the type who would do something like this?"

"The guy's a crook. He basically got his company by swindling someone else out of it. He'd almost drained it dry by the time Bryan moved in to take it over. Childers's name has been connected with several crimes—mail fraud, embezzlement, that sort of thing—but there's never been enough evidence to bring him up on charges. Yeah, he's the type who would do this."

"Do you—?"

He looked at her when he faltered. "Do I what?"

"Do you think they ever intended to let us go?"

Donovan's eyes held hers for a moment, and then he looked away.

He had never lied to her, Chloe mused. He simply chose not to answer some of her questions. And maybe that was just as well.

Still, she felt the need to ask just one more question. "Do you think Bryan will find us?"

He answered that one without hesitation. "He'll find us."

"You seem to have a lot of confidence in him."

"I do," he answered simply.

"I hope you're right."

After a few more minutes of listening to the rain fall, Donovan stirred. "How are your feet?"

"Numb. I can't really feel them right now."

"Still thirsty?"

"Not enough to go out in the rain," she answered with a faint smile.

"I'd go get you some water, but I don't have anything to carry it in."

He was so determined to take care of her. A bit wistfully, she found herself wondering if it was only because it was his job to do so. "That's okay."

"I wish I had something for you to eat. I guess we could chew on some acorns or something."

That made her laugh. "No, thanks. I'm not quite that hungry yet."

"You have a nice laugh," he murmured, his gaze on her smiling mouth.

Her smile immediately froze.

Donovan looked away. "Uh—Bryan thinks so, too. He mentioned it when he first told me about you."

Bryan. The name slid between them like an invisible wall.

Funny. Chloe could hardly bring Bryan's face to her mind at the moment.

The rain eventually slowed and then stopped. Chloe inched to the cave opening to peer out again. Water dripped steadily off the leaves of the branches that nearly obscured their hideaway. Swollen by the downpour, the stream ran more swiftly than before. A deer and her fawn drank downstream, then turned and disappeared gracefully into the trees. The sky was still low and gray, but the rain seemed to have ended for a while.

Under any other circumstances, Chloe might have been enjoying this encounter with unspoiled nature.

She wasn't surprised when Donovan said, "We should get moving. Before it starts raining again."

Though it wasn't easy, she noddcd. "I'm ready."

"You're sure you can walk?"

That brought her chin up. "I can walk."

"It's going to be wet. Slippery in places."

"I'll be careful."

He placed a hand on her arm when she started to rise. "Chloe—I'm sorry this happened to you. You don't deserve this."

"Neither do you. So let's get going."

His mouth quirked. "Right behind you, General."

His rare flashes of humor always caught her off guard. With a chuckle, she let him help her to her feet. Resisting an impulse to curse against the pain that shot up from her feet, she fell into step behind Donovan.

Ten steps at a time, she told herself. She would make this journey ten steps at a time.

Chapter Seven

Cold waves of anger poured off the black-haired man behind the desk, seemingly lowering the temperature in the room a good ten degrees. Bryan Falcon didn't lose his temper very often—but when he did, the people around him usually ducked for cover.

Jason Colby didn't duck, but he kept his voice as soothing as possible as he completed the report. "We had a possible sighting last night of the van the witness at the diner reported seeing at the same time Donovan and Chloe disappeared. It was reported speeding in north-central Arkansas by a state trooper who lost sight of it after it took a series of sharp turns on twisting side roads. That's also the general area to which we traced the ransom call. There are dozens of hunting cabins and isolated rural buildings where they could be hiding. If they haven't moved on, of course."

Falcon studied his security officer through narrowed, midnight-blue eyes. "We'll assume for now that they have not. It wouldn't be easy to take Donovan in the first place, much less to keep moving him around, so we'll concentrate the search in that area."

"The St. Francis National Forest covers about a million acres, but I think we can narrow it down more than that. I've marked off several search grids, and the teams have already been set into motion."

"I want them found, Jason."

"Yes, sir."

"In the meantime, I'll keep stalling the callers. They're supposed to contact me again tomorrow. I asked for twenty-four hours to get the ransom together without arousing media suspicion."

Jason frowned. "They didn't argue with you?"

"The guy made a show of blustering and threatening me, but yeah, they gave it to me."

"Interesting."

"Exactly what I thought. Why do you think the guy would sound almost relieved about a delay?"

"Problems on their end."

"Maybe."

Jason cleared his throat and phrased his next question very carefully. "Is it possible that they're willing to stall—because something has happened to their hostages?"

The only change in his boss's expression was the muscle that jumped in his clenched jaw. "Just keep looking for them."

Because Jason had known Bryan long enough to recognize the genuine pain behind the stern control, he nodded and rose quickly to his feet. "We'll find them, Bryan."

Bryan stared at him without really seeing him. "Yes, we'll find them."

He would accept no other possibility.

The rain didn't hold off for long. Donovan and Chloe had been walking maybe an hour when it started again. They ducked under a jutting bluff for cover, but it provided little protection, and both of them got pretty wet. Chloe tried to hide her shivering from Donovan, but she suspected he knew she was cold. He just didn't mention it because there was nothing he could do about it except keep her moving, which he did as soon as the rain stopped a second time.

She was thirsty again, and so hungry that her stomach rumbled and her head ached. She wanted a cold glass of water; a nice, long shower; a hot meal and a soft bed—in that order. And a toothbrush, she added, running her tongue over her teeth. She'd done her best to rinse her mouth and finger-scrub her teeth at the stream they were following through the forest, but she wanted a toothbrush and her favorite mint-flavored toothpaste.

In a futile attempt to distract herself from her discomfort, she made an effort to concentrate on the beauty of nature—which meant trying to ignore the heavy gray sky crowding down on them. Had there been sunshine, the spring leaves would have been a soft, fresh green. The hills and steep valleys were dotted with dogwoods and redbuds in full bloom. She saw an occasional bird or squirrel, but most of the wildlife seemed to be holed up from the dismal weather.

She'd taken her eyes off her feet while she surveyed the area. She tripped over a thick vine, and for once Donovan wasn't fast enough to catch her. She went down hard, landing on her hands and knees.

He was beside her instantly. "Are you all right?"

Embarrassed, she straightened, brushing mud and wet leaves off her hands. "I'm fine."

"Let me see." He took her hands in his, turning her palms up so he could examine them. Fortunately, the ground was still soft from the rain and only her pride had been injured in the fall. The knees of her khaki slacks were damp and filthy now, but the fabric had protected her skin.

Still cradling her hands in his, Donovan frowned down at her. "Can you walk?"

"Of course I can walk." She rolled her eyes. "I just stumbled, Donovan. I'm fine, really."

His face had settled into the rock-hard mask he used to conceal his emotions, but she recognized the glint of anger in his eyes. Though he was still a mystery to her in many ways, she was getting to know him better now. Well enough to know that he was blaming himself for letting her fall. Typical of him.

"You shouldn't have to be going through this," he muttered. "When we get out of here and I get my hands on the people behind this...."

She squeezed his hands gently with her muddied ones. "We'll get out," she said confidently. "And then you can take steps to get justice for what we've been through—legally, of course."

She didn't quite catch his growl of response, but she had a feeling he wasn't too concerned about the legality of the revenge he was plotting.

"Let's keep walking," she suggested. "I'll be more careful."

They moved onward, but this time Donovan was never more than an arm's length away from her. Chloe was both annoyed and reluctantly amused by his obvious assumption that she could hardly take care of herself. She noted that his steps were slowing, too, and that he was limping almost as badly as she was. She took no pleasure in his discomfort, but she focused on it occasionally to remind herself that if he could keep going, she could, too.

She glanced up at the sky, noting that it looked as though the rain could start again at any minute. As if to confirm her prediction, a single fat drop landed on her cheek, sliding off her chin. "How long do you think it's been since we left the cave?"

"I don't know. Maybe four hours. We've got a few more hours until dark."

"We've walked so far. It seems like we'd have come across some sign of civilization."

"Didn't you read about that little girl who was lost in a forest in north Arkansas a year or so ago? She simply slipped away from her grandparents during an outing, and it took hundreds of searchers three or four days to find her. Even then it took the men who found her nearly six hours to return her to her family—and they were riding mules. The forest is big and dense, and the terrain so uneven that it's easy to get lost here and hard to be found."

She swallowed. For once, Donovan had told her more than she wanted to know. She took some comfort in remembering that the child had been unharmed when she was found, even after several nights and days with no food.

She tucked her head and kept moving, looking only at her feet now. She wouldn't risk falling again—and there was nothing ahead except more trees and bluffs. Occasionally, Donovan helped her up a steep incline or over a log or across a large, mossy boulder that blocked their way, but for the most part they traveled in silence.

They were walking along a ridge of rock so narrow that they had to go single-file when Donovan came to a stop so abruptly that she nearly barreled into him. "What is it?" she asked, craning to see around him.

"A cabin. More of a lean-to, actually."

She was looking in the same direction he was, toward a heavy tangle of brush on the other side of a deep, erosion-carved crevasse. Water ran through the crevasse—the same stream they'd been more or less following all day. She didn't see any sign of a building. "Where?"

"There." He nodded toward the heaviest section of brush. "It's almost covered with vines, but it's there."

She thought she saw it now, a rickety structure made of boards and metal. "Abandoned," she said with a sigh. No help there.

"Maybe." His whole body alert, Donovan seemed to be studying the area intently. Warily.

She lifted her eyebrows. "What are you looking for?"

"That shelter probably belongs to someone who grows illegal crops in the nearest clearing. It's fairly common in areas this isolated."

"Marijuana?" Chloe whispered, her eyes wide.

He nodded.

"Do you think they're still here?" Shrinking back into the shadow of a tree behind her, she looked around for crazed drug growers with shotguns.

She was relieved when Donovan shook his head. "I think the shelter's been abandoned. I don't see any signs of recent activity. It's still too cool outside for agricultural activities, anyway."

A sudden, exciting thought occurred to her, making her clutch Donovan's arm. "There must be a road that leads to civilization from here. Whoever built this shelter had to have a way to get here."

"There's probably an old logging road or a rough trail of some sort nearby," he agreed, looking as though he'd already considered that possibility.

"We can follow it out."

"We'll have to be careful, but that's exactly what we'll do."

He moved toward the shelter and she started to follow, but he motioned for her to remain where she was. "I want to check the place out. You wait here until I'm sure it's safe."

"What are you expecting to find?"

He shrugged. "If we're lucky—nothing. But there could be animals. Or booby traps."

She moistened her lips. "Booby traps?"

"Drug farmers are notoriously paranoid about being raided by the feds. It's not at all uncommon for them to rig primitive but effective security systems."

"But what if you—"

"I know what to look for," he interrupted, speaking over his shoulder. "Stay put. This won't take long."

Chewing her lip, she sank to the ground beneath the big tree, knowing she was fairly well hidden in the shadows. It felt good to sit again, but she couldn't relax because she worried about Donovan blundering into a dangerous situation.

Not that Donovan ever seemed to "blunder," she mentally amended. She'd never met anyone who seemed more competent, more fully in control. Though she hadn't truly felt safe since they'd been kidnapped in that parking lot—was it really just over twenty-four hours ago?—she'd trusted Donovan to take care of her, and he had. Their captors had greatly underestimated him. She didn't make that mistake.

What had he done, she wondered, to make him an expert on primitive booby traps? Or opening handcuffs with hairpins? Or hand-to-hand combat?

He had told her he entered the military straight out of high school, and there had been a gap between his leaving the military and going to work for Bryan. He'd been evasive about what he'd done during those years. Chloe couldn't help but be curious now.

Donovan wasn't out of her sight for long. Emerging from the brush-covered lean-to, he strode toward the shallow ravine that separated them. He looked satisfied, she decided. Apparently his search had revealed no dangers.

"It's clear," he said, still several yards away from her. "And even better—I found food."

"Food?" She pushed herself to her feet, her stomach growling in anticipation. "Did you say food?"

Still making his way toward her, he nodded. "Some canned fruit, a few canned vegetables. The cans are dusty, but intact. They haven't been here too long—probably since last summer. It should be safe to—"

The words were cut off when he stepped unsuspectingly into a deep hole just before he reached the crevasse. His right leg disappeared to the knee, and he went down hard. His choked cry of pain brought her heart into her throat as she ran toward him, her socks sliding on the damp ground. "Donovan? Are you all right?"

"It's my leg," he answered through clenched teeth, holding his right leg with both hands.

"Your leg?" She knelt beside him, one hand on his back. "Do you think it's broken?"

"I think there's a good chance. *Damn* it."

Apparently he'd stepped into a sinkhole created by soft dirt being washed away from an area of rocks and tree limbs. The heavy rain that morning had softened the ground around the hole, letting it give way when he'd set his foot down. A sharp-edged rock had sliced into his pants leg, and blood made a large, dark splotch on the fabric.

"Oh, my God." She helped him stretch the injured leg in front of him, and then knelt beside it to examine the damage. Pulling the torn fabric out of the way, she was relieved to determine that the cut wasn't deep, though it was bleeding steadily. Nor had broken bone punctured the skin. She couldn't feel a break when she ran her fingertips lightly over his shin, but that didn't mean the bone wasn't cracked. Without an X-ray, there was no way to tell for certain.

"We need to stop this bleeding first." She pulled off her denim shirt, then reached for the hem of her coral T-shirt. "Turn your head."

Though his face was pale and his mouth set in a tight line of pain, Donovan still managed a quizzical look at her. "I beg your pardon?"

"We need fabric for a bandage. I have an extra shirt, so turn your head." No way was she stripping to her undies with him looking. He wasn't hurt *that* badly.

When she was sure he was looking away, she pulled the T-shirt over her head. The cool, damp air swept her skin, tightening her nipples beneath her thin cotton bra and making goose bumps parade down her arms. She snatched up her denim shirt and shoved her arms into the sleeves, drawing it snugly around her. She'd lost a button at some point, but she fastened the ones that remained.

She took the T-shirt in both hands and pulled, trying to rip it. She discovered a moment later that she had invested in a very high-quality fabric. Though it stretched, it wouldn't tear. She muttered a mild curse and tried again.

Donovan reached out to take the shirt from her hands. A few efficient pulls and he had the shirt in shreds.

She sighed and accepted the coral strips from him. "Thank you."

Fortunately, his black pants fit loosely, so she was able to push the right leg up and out of the way. The cut looked clean, and the edges even, so she wrapped one strip of fabric around his leg and tied it securely.

"That should keep the cut clean, anyway," she murmured. "Now what are we going to do about the break?"

He'd made a visible effort to force his pain aside and speak without any show of emotion. "We'll splint it. I saw some short boards lying next to the cabin—probably left over from when it was built. We can use a couple of those to brace my leg and keep the bone from moving if it is broken. We'll secure them with strips of cloth. It won't be ideal, but maybe it'll brace my leg when I walk. I'll rig up some crutches or something to help bear my weight."

She frowned at him. "You're not planning to start walking again?"

"We aren't going to fly out of here."

"Donovan, you can't hike when your leg could be broken."

"Chloe, I have no choice."

"That's crazy."

"Just find some narrow boards to use for the splint, will you?"

Muttering deprecations about foolishly macho men, Chloe searched the small pile of rotting wood for usable boards. She found two that were roughly two feet long and four inches wide, each about an inch thick. Definitely not ideal—but all she had at the moment. Stumbling over the occasional rock or twig—and promising herself she would never step foot outside without her shoes again—she carried them back to where he waited.

With Donovan's help, she splinted his lower leg tightly. Already it was beginning to swell, and she worried that they could be causing more damage than they were preventing, but he refused to listen to her concerns. He fully intended to keep walking as soon as he was upright again, and there didn't seem to be anything she could do to talk him out of it.

"At least rest a few minutes before we start again. You said there was some food in the cabin. We should eat something if it looks safe. And besides," she added as thunder made itself heard in the distance, "it's going to rain again soon."

He nodded. "Help me up."

Wedging her shoulder under his arm, she supported him as he rose, keeping his weight on his left foot. She served as his crutch while they made their way to the shelter. The swinging handcuff bracelet bumped her upper arm, but she ignored it. He was heavy, but he spared her his full weight, hopping on his good foot until they reached the building—which really was more lean-to than cabin.

They ducked through the small door that dangled precariously on its hinges. The inside of the tiny building was dark and dusty, little light filtering in through the one small glass pane set into the back wall. The only furnishings were a couple of rickety chairs, a dust-covered table, and what appeared to be a wood-framed bed covered with a heavy tarp. Against one wall was a rough countertop littered with abandoned supplies—a broken lantern, several stacks of cans, and a box filled with assorted tools and utensils.

Chloe helped Donovan into one of the chairs, caught her breath for a moment, then moved toward the counter. There was no sink for washing any of the dirty items. Nor was there a stove of any sort. "How do you suppose he cooked?"

"Probably on a portable camp stove—maybe a campfire, though he wouldn't risk much smoke in case of DEA planes flying over."

She found a battered metal saucepan, the bottom scorched black with soot, sitting upside down on the counter. "I'll bring water in from the stream to wash a couple of utensils so we can eat."

"Be careful."

"I will." Carrying the saucepan, she went back outside to the stream. Kneeling beside the stream, she dipped the pan into the water, then drew a deep breath and closed her eyes for a moment, her shoulders sagging.

She hadn't wanted to fall apart in front of Donovan, but she was beginning to despair that they would ever be rescued. They were stranded in a remote cabin probably owned by drug dealers, miles from anywhere, with three armed men on their trail. Donovan's leg could be broken, and she suspected that her bloodied feet were becoming infected. Even if Bryan had been contacted by their kidnappers, he had no way to know where they were now, couldn't possibly be looking for them here.

Maybe they should have stayed where they were. Who was to say that they wouldn't have been released, unharmed, after Bryan paid the ransom? What made Donovan so certain their safety had depended on escape?

She drew a deep breath and forced her shoulders straight. They *had* escaped, and now Donovan was hurt, waiting inside for her to return. He'd been so conscientious about taking care of her; the least she could do was return the favor now.

She scrubbed the pan as best she could with sand, gravel and stream water. When it was as clean as she could manage, she filled it with water and carried it back to the cabin. There was a pinhole leak in the bottom of the pan. Drops of water oozed out of it, but slowly enough that it didn't concern her much.

Donovan was still in the chair, his head back, his eyes closed, his shackled right hand resting on the thigh of his outstretched, injured leg. It was the second time since she'd met him that he looked even slightly vulnerable. The first had been when he'd lain unconscious in that van, his head resting on her lap.

She ran a hand through her damp hair and cleared her throat. "I brought water."

He opened his eyes and straightened, apparently embarrassed to be caught giving in to his weakness for even a moment. "No problems?"

"None. Would you like to lie down on the cot? I can help you—"

"I'd like to eat," he cut in gruffly. "Do you see a can opener over there?"

He was making it quite clear that he didn't want her hovering over him. She carried the box full of tools and utensils to the table and rummaged through it until she found an old-fashioned can opener—along with a few other things that would definitely come in handy. Two partially-burned candles and a box of matches were an especially welcome sight, since it was growing darker every minute in the cabin as the dark clouds gathered again outside. The sight of an unopened bar of soap still in its original wrapper was almost as welcome a discovery as the food.

Dipping the can opener in the pan of water to clean it as best as she could, she turned to the half-dozen cans stacked in one corner of the counter. A fat beetle waddled across the counter top when she poked at the cans, and there was a rustling in the far corner of the cabin that could only be mice—but she put squeamishness out of her mind and concentrated on the food. A large, undented can of fruit cocktail, the label faded but clearly readable, seemed the best bet.

There were no plates, but she scrubbed a couple of dented forks, then set the opened can of fruit in front of Donovan. "You're sure it's safe to eat this?"

He studied the contents, sniffed them, then nodded. "As long as the can was intact, there should be no problem. Trust me, I've eaten worse."

"If you say so."

He offered her the can again. "Go ahead. Have what you want and I'll finish the rest."

"You eat first," she said, turning toward the soap. "I'm going out to the stream to wash up a bit."

"That sounds good. Maybe I'll hobble out to the stream after I've eaten."

"Why don't I bring water back in here, instead?" she countered, picking up the saucepan she'd used earlier, and adding it to the soap and extra strip of T-shirt fabric she already held. "I'd like you to stay off that leg for a little while."

He shrugged. "The longer I wait to get back on my feet, the harder it's going to be when we have to start moving again."

"Still, it won't hurt you to rest some first." She opened the creaky cabin door. "I won't be long."

"Just be careful."

Nodding, she slipped outside.

The sky was so overcast that it looked like twilight, even though she knew nighttime was still officially a couple hours away. Hoping the rain would hold off just a little longer, she set the pan, the scrap of fabric and the soap beside the stream and unbuttoned her shirt.

She wasn't one to strip outside, but she absolutely had to wash. And it wasn't as if there was anyone around to see her, anyway. She only wished she had clean clothes to put on when she finished.

Wearing nothing but her ragged socks, she waded into the shallow, fast-running stream, being very careful not to lose her balance. Kneeling, she used the soap and cloth to scrub herself. She used the pan to scoop water over her hair, which she washed as best she could with the hard bar of soap. She was freezing—her teeth chattering, her skin covered with goose bumps—but she was determined to be as clean as she could get under the circumstances.

She put her clothes back on over wet skin—not a particularly pleasant feeling, but at least they helped warm her a little. Turning the pan upside down, she used it as a little stool so she wouldn't have to sit directly in the mud while she turned her attention to her feet. The wet, shredded socks were somewhat cleaner now and she was able to peel them away from her scabbed feet with only a little hissing and cursing.

Her feet looked awful—bruised, torn, scraped, swollen—but she reminded herself that Donovan was hurt worse. She washed them gently, trying to ignore the pain, concentrating on how good it felt just to be clean.

She didn't really want to put the wet socks back on, but she didn't want to walk barefoot to the cabin, either. She turned the socks upside down so that the relatively undamaged parts were on the bottom to provide some protection for the soles of her feet. Wrinkling her nose at the squishy, soggy feel of wet socks against damp ground, she filled the pan with water and headed back to the cabin.

She was wet, cold, hungry and tired—but Donovan needed her.

Chapter Eight

From his chair at the table, Donovan looked up when Chloe reentered the cabin. He decided right then it was a good thing their unwitting landlord wasn't vain enough to keep a mirror in the cabin. Because he had already discovered that Chloe was fastidious when it came to her cleanliness and appearance, he knew she would be appalled if she could see herself at that moment.

Her hair was wet and slicked close to her head, her denim shirt was wrinkled, dirty and missing a button in the middle, her khaki slacks were liberally splashed with mud and grass-stained at the knees. Her lips were a bit blue from the cold, and there were dark smudges beneath her eyes. She still limped with every step. But he was pleased to note that she didn't look quite as pale and worn-out as she had earlier.

"Your bath must have revived you a bit," he commented.

"It feels so much better to be clean—at least cleaner than I was," she amended, approaching the table.

Her eyes widened when she saw the handcuffs lying next to the half-full can of fruit. The silver metal gleamed in the dim, flickering light of the candle Donovan had set in the middle of the table. "You got the cuffs off."

He nodded and unconsciously rubbed his right wrist. "I found a few usable tools in the box of junk."

"You had to walk over to the counter to get the candle and the matches. Honestly, Donovan, you could have fallen again or reinjured your leg. Why didn't you wait for me?"

"Because it was getting too dark to see in here. And I needed to find out if I could walk on my own."

He thought it best not to mention that he'd also peeked out the door, just to make sure she was all right. He hadn't liked having her out of his sight for that long. What he'd seen had caused him to spend the short time that had passed since getting his stubborn and uncooperative body back under control.

He couldn't recall ever seeing anything more beautiful than Chloe standing unselfconsciously nude in that stream, a gracefully feminine cameo against the heavy gray clouds. It was a vision he would remember for a long time, one he expected to see quite often in his dreams.

Pushing the appealing image out of his mind for the moment, he nudged the can of fruit toward her. "You must be hungry now. Have the rest of this fruit."

Still shaking her head in disapproval at his stubborn refusal to baby his leg, she moved to the other chair. She sank into it slowly, then nearly pitched sideways out of it when the chair wobbled sharply on uneven legs. She steadied herself quickly.

He'd started to move to catch her, but relaxed again when it was obvious that she didn't need his assistance. "Okay?"

She bent to peer beneath the seat of her chair. "Looks like you're not the only one in this room with a broken leg," she murmured, then seemed to immediately regret the flippant words, judging by her self-recriminating expression.

He chuckled, wryly amused rather than offended. They might as well try to find some humor about their situation. It sure beat whining and griping, which wouldn't have benefited either of them. And he was greatly relieved that Chloe hadn't yet succumbed to tears. There was nothing that discomfited him more than a crying woman.

"Eat," he said. "The fruit tastes pretty good."

She picked up a fork with a weary smile. "I'm sure it does. But I'm almost too tired to chew."

But she ate, anyway, and seemed to enjoy the simple fare. She had to have been as hungry as he'd been earlier.

She hadn't even finished eating before the sky opened up again. Rain hammered noisily against the metal room. There were leaks, of course, but nothing too problematic.

In resignation, Donovan figured they might as well spend the rest of the night here and head out again at dawn. They would follow what little excuse for a road they could find, and hope that they found help before anyone dangerous found them.

He was certainly in no shape to defend himself and Chloe against at least three adversaries now.

Except for the sound of the rain, it was quiet in the cabin. Donovan couldn't think of much to say as he rubbed his still-chafed right wrist and glared at his injured leg. It still throbbed from his activity earlier, and he could see that there was some swelling beneath the makeshift splint, but he didn't think the break was too bad if it was broken. Cracked, maybe.

At least the bone didn't seem to have shattered, and hadn't punctured the skin. He'd broken bones before, and he knew this injury was more worrisome than dangerous, but he was still furious with himself for allowing it to happen.

How many more stupid mistakes could he make in front of Chloe? He'd been screwing up since she'd first gotten into his car, finally resulting in her being in this dismal position. He'd bet she never wanted to see him again once they got out of this mess. And he *would* get her out. Or die trying.

It had been well over twenty-four hours since they'd been taken. Donovan had no doubt that Bryan had already mobilized an extensive search, which would begin at the diner where they'd abandoned the car. Jason Colby, Falcon's head of security, would be leading the search—and he was the best. If there had been any witnesses—anyone at all who'd seen the van near his car—Jason and Bryan would find them.

Because he knew them both so well, and because they'd trained and prepared for eventualities like this one, Donovan knew exactly what procedures Jason and Bryan would be following now. The entire area within driving distance of the diner would be marked into sections and teams dispatched to each. Bryan would spare no money or resources for the search—and he had plenty of each. He would be furious—and he wouldn't rest until he knew Donovan and Chloe were safe.

Chloe set the empty can aside, the movement drawing his attention back to her. He was beginning to strongly doubt now that Bryan's selection of a potential mate had been as calculated and cold-hearted as he'd led Donovan to believe.

Bryan had insisted that he'd chosen Chloe because of her qualifications as a potential wife and mother, and Donovan acknowledged those traits now. She was intelligent, competent, composed, resourceful—and stronger than she looked. She'd kept her head during this crisis; he knew plenty of women—and a few men—who would be in hysterics by now. Not once had she complained during the long, difficult night, even though her tender feet had been shredded by the nearly barefoot hike.

But there was more to admire about Chloe, he had to acknowledge. The way her hazel eyes reflected her emotions. The tiny dimples that flirted around the corners of her mouth when she smiled. The graceful sway of her hips when she walked. The silkiness of her hair, the softness of her skin. Her slender waist that emphasized the nice curves of her breasts and hips. Her long, shapely legs.

Since his friend was neither blind nor stupid, Donovan had no doubt that Bryan was aware of those physical attributes.

Donovan was becoming entirely too aware of them himself.

He watched as she smothered a yawn behind her hand. He started to rise, using a heavy stick he'd found propped in a corner for a cane.

Chloe moved to stop him. "What are you doing? If you need something, I'll get it for you."

"I'm just checking out the bed. Maybe it's reasonably clean since it's been covered with a tarp."

"The mattress is probably disgusting."

But they discovered when he pulled off the dirty tarp that there *was* no mattress. The homemade, full-bed-sized cot was made army style, consisting of a heavy wooden frame over which had been stretched a strong green canvas hammock. The canvas was faded and slightly frayed in spots, but looked relatively clean and sturdy.

"It's not too bad," he said, studying the primitive structure. "Certainly as clean as the cave we slept in last night. Why don't you try to get some rest?"

She eyed the bed warily. "You're the one who needs to lie down," she replied. "You shouldn't be standing on that leg. You must be in so much pain."

"It's not too bad," he lied.

It was obvious that she didn't believe him. She glanced toward the cluttered countertop. "I wonder if there's any chance of finding a painkiller among that mess."

Donovan chuckled. "I don't believe I want any of the drugs you'd find in here, thanks."

She wrinkled her nose at him, an expression he found particularly enticing. "I meant an aspirin. Or some other over-the-counter medication, obviously."

Still smiling a little, he shook his head. "I'll be okay."

She looked again at the bed. "I doubt that this cot

is going to be particularly comfortable for you. But then, neither was that cave, I suppose—especially since you had to sit upright all night.''

''I've slept in worse positions.''

Moving toward the cot, she cocked an eyebrow at him. ''Someday I'd like to hear more about your past adventures.''

That comment made his slight smile fade. Though he knew she was mostly teasing, he couldn't respond in the same light tone. There were still too many raw wounds from his adventurous past that were barely scabbed over. He'd rather deal with a broken leg any day rather than have those old emotional wounds examined.

Apparently, she had learned not to expect a response to everything she said to him. Without waiting for him to speak, she motioned toward the bed. ''You first. I want you off that leg.''

''Actually, I'd like to wash up first. You seemed to feel a lot better after your bath, and I'm pretty grubby myself.''

That argument obviously made sense to her. ''Of course you want to wash. It really does feel better to be clean.''

She hesitated a moment, then sat on the edge of the cot. ''I'll turn my back. Unless you need my help, of course.''

He felt his mouth kick into another slight smile, though the thought of having Chloe help him bathe was anything but humorous to him. ''I can handle it. And I'm not really modest.''

It was hard to tell in the deep shadows, but he thought her cheeks went pink before she lay on the cot and turned her back to him. ''*I* am,'' she muttered.

Definitely a good thing he hadn't mentioned checking on her while she was bathing, he decided wryly, tugging his grubby black shirt over his head. He had to drag his gaze away from the sight of Chloe's nicely rounded bottom as he turned to pick up the soap.

She never glanced around as he washed as best he could under the circumstances, using the leaking pan of cold water, the hard bar of soap, and the last dry scrap from the T-shirt. When he was finished and fully dressed again, he pulled the two chairs close together.

"What are you doing now?" she asked, turning around when she heard the chairs scraping against the wooden floor.

He had come to the conclusion that it would be much better if he didn't climb into a bed—not even this sorry excuse for one—with Chloe. "The cot's not really big enough to hold both of us comfortably. I'll sit in one chair and prop my legs on the other. You get some sleep, I'll be fine."

Frowning, she wriggled into a sitting position on the cot. "There's no way I can rest on our only bed while you're sitting in that awful chair with a broken leg. You, I mean, not the chair. Well, both you *and* the chair. Oh, you know what I mean."

He couldn't help smiling again at her disjointed tirade. Funny how often she made him smile, even under these circumstances. "I told you, I'm—"

"Look, this cot is bigger than it looks. There's room for both of us to get some sleep if we're still."

The only way they would fit was to lie pressed together. And that position would most likely drive him insane by daylight. "I don't think we should—"

She didn't let him finish. "Come on, I slept with my head in your lap last night. It's no big deal."

Because he could still very clearly remember the feel of her head on his thigh, her cheek resting close to a very sensitive area—not to mention the sight of her bathing in that stream—he was even more certain he should stay right where he was. "I—uh—"

She stood. After waiting for a rolling grumble of thunder to end, she said firmly, "This storm could go on all night. There's no chance we'll be able to leave before daylight, and little chance that anyone will find us here. If you're really crazy enough to try hiking again tomorrow, you're going to have to get some rest first. And I can't sleep unless I know you do."

She had a stubborn set to her mouth that told him she wasn't going to listen to argument. She was fully prepared to sit up all night if he did argue.

The thought of climbing onto that narrow bed with her was unsettling—but he *was* tired. And, hell, with his leg in a splint, there wasn't much he could do with her in that bed, anyway…not that she'd had anything like that in mind when she'd invited him over, of course.

Since she needed rest and swore she couldn't until he did, he would practically be doing her a favor to get into bed with her.

Satisfied with his logic, he nodded and reached for the stick again.

She sprang to his side. "Let me help you."

It had become apparent to him that Chloe was more comfortable taking care of someone else than she was being cared for. He paused to blow out the candle, plunging the room into near-darkness, then allowed her to assist him to the bed. He motioned for her to take the inside, next to the wall. And then he sat on the edge and lifted his legs carefully onto the cot, his right leg on the outside edge.

It was a close fit, as he had expected, but not much tighter than the cave had been the night before. There were no pillows, of course, so he was lying flat on his back, as was Chloe. Pressed side to side, they lay so still and stiff they could have been plastic mannequins.

This was ridiculous, he thought. Neither of them would get any sleep this way.

"Relax," he advised her. "You won't bother me if you move."

"Donovan?" Her voice was very quiet in the darkness.

He bent his right arm under his head, staring up at the rain-hammered metal roof. "Mm?"

"How far do you think we are from civilization?"

"Don't know. I figure it's quite a way, since the guy who built this place obviously didn't care for company. It's probably an all-day drive with a four-wheel-drive vehicle."

"And how long walking?"

"More than a day." Especially with his leg broken, he added silently.

"How *much* more?"

"I don't know."

After a brief silence, she asked in a small voice, "Are you ever afraid that we *won't* get out?"

For the first time since they'd gotten away from their kidnappers, Chloe sounded scared. Vulnerable. She needed comforting—and while he wasn't very good at that sort of thing, he would do his best.

He shifted his weight, then slid his left arm beneath

her and pulled her onto his shoulder. "We'll get out," he said gruffly. "It's just a matter of not giving up."

Her hand on his chest, she burrowed into his shoulder as if grateful for the contact. But her voice was steady when she said, "I'm not giving up. I just wondered if you ever have any doubts."

"I'm only human, Chloe." Human enough to have a decidedly physical reaction to her nestling against him—but he pushed that awareness to the back of his mind and continued, "I can't help wondering if something else will go wrong. Believe me, I've thought of every bad scenario that could happen to us—from wild animal attacks to a fall from one of those bluffs. But we can't let fear paralyze us if we're going to survive."

He was half afraid his impulsive admission of weakness might increase her anxiety. Instead, she said, "It's kind of nice to know you're worried about those things, too. It makes me feel a little less cowardly."

"Cowardly?" He shook his head against the canvas beneath him. "Chloe, you're one of the least cowardly people I've ever met, man or woman. After all we've been through, I wouldn't blame you if you were a basket case by now, but you've handled everything that's come our way without complaining once."

He wasn't usually one to lavish praise, but he thought she should know he admired her courage and resilience.

There were a lot of things he admired about Chloe Pennington.

"Has anyone ever told you that you can be very sweet?" she asked after a rather lengthy pause.

He couldn't see her face in the darkness, of course, but he knew she was smiling up at him. "*Sweet* isn't a description I've heard very often," he muttered wryly, though he was pleased to note that she sounded more at ease now.

"That's because you come across so tough. But I want you to know how much I appreciate the way you've taken such good care of me throughout this ordeal." Stretching upward, she brushed a light kiss against his jaw.

The contact jolted him like an electric shock, coursing through his veins and spilling into his groin. His arm tightened reflexively around her, but he forced himself to loosen his grip.

It was only gratitude, he reminded himself. And gratitude was all he had a right to accept from her.

"Go to sleep," he said, his voice more curt than he had intended. "We've got a long day ahead tomorrow."

He might have expected her to be rebuffed by his tone—or at least a tad annoyed. Instead, she laughed softly and burrowed more cozily into his shoulder. "G'night, Donovan."

Grunting a response, he stared up at the rain-pounded metal roof and prepared for another near-sleepless night.

It was early Wednesday—before 8:00 a.m.—when Bryan Falcon knocked on Grace Pennington's door. He'd called first, so he knew she would be expecting him. But he was still a bit startled by how quickly she threw open the door.

"Good morn—" he began.

"Where's my sister?" she cut in, glaring at him.

It always amazed him that Chloe and Grace were identical in appearance, yet so different in personality. Chloe was calm, courteous and serene, while Grace was impatient, impulsive and quick-tempered.

He wasn't looking forward to the next few minutes. "May I come in?"

She moved aside, then barely allowed him time to step into the converted warehouse, loft-style apartment before she asked again, "Where's my sister?"

He motioned toward the colorful, contemporary furniture arranged invitingly around the big, airy room. "Maybe we should sit down."

"You're avoiding my question." She planted her feet and fisted her hands on her hips. "I'm starting to lose patience with you."

Patience? He wasn't aware that she possessed any.

As wary as he was of her temper, he softened when he saw the genuine fear reflected in her hazel eyes. She was doing her best to bluster and intimidate him, but, truth was, she knew something was wrong with Chloe—and she was terrified.

Because he could understand those feelings, and because he shared them, he was able to keep his expression pleasant. "We need to talk, Grace."

Her throat moved with a hard swallow. "Just tell me," she whispered. "Is she all right?"

He set his hands on her shoulders and turned her gently toward a bright purple couch.

"Sit," he said, speaking more firmly now to penetrate the fog of fear that seemed to grip her. "I'll tell you everything I know at this point."

Donovan must have been more tired than he had realized. Though he hadn't expected to sleep, he did. Heavily.

The dirty porthole of a window allowed enough sun to seep through that he could tell it was midmorning when he finally opened his eyes. Nine, maybe even ten o'clock, he surmised, startled by the realization. He never slept that late, no matter how tired he was.

It must have been a combination of exhaustion, pain and the dim light in the cabin that had lulled him into sleeping for so long—not to mention the pleasure of having a warm, soft body snuggled against his, he thought, turning his attention to Chloe. He felt her stir, and sensed with a touch of regret that she was waking. They would have to start hiking again soon.

Who would have thought he would find himself reluctant to leave this shabby excuse for a cabin?

She opened her eyes and blinked up at him, taking a moment to orient herself. And then she gave him a sleepy smile that brought out the little dimples at the corners of her mouth. "Good morning."

Her voice was sleep-husky, her tone intimate. The sound of it did things to him that he was best not thinking of at the moment. He shifted his hips a bit, pulling away from her just far enough that she wouldn't become aware of just how pleasant he found it to awaken with her.

"Good morning," he said, making an effort to keep his own voice brusque. "Sleep well?"

"Mm-hmm." Still obviously half-asleep, she stretched like a lazy cat, the movement brushing her against him again.

Much more of this, he decided, and he was going to explode. He turned away from her, reaching for the stick he'd left on the floor beside the bed. "I'll see what sort of fruit we're having for breakfast."

"Don't suppose you can stir up some coffee while you're at it?" she asked around a yawn as she, too, rose to a sitting position.

"I wish." He'd just about break his other leg for a steaming mug of coffee, but since that wasn't an option at the moment, he put it out of his mind and limped to the counter.

His leg was bruised and swollen, so sore it required effort not to wince with every step. He knew there was a risk of infection with every break, even simple ones, but he hoped an infection would at least hold off until he and Chloe could walk to safety.

Hearing Chloe moving around behind him, he stood at the counter mentally preparing for the next stage of their journey. His gaze fell on the box of matches they'd left lying on the counter the night before. He slipped that and a small knife into one deep trouser pocket.

He wouldn't be able to carry much and still keep his weight off his leg, but he'd take what he could. They would rig up something in which to carry the remaining few cans of fruit. He figured they had a couple of days of hiking ahead of them—if they were lucky and he led them in the right direction—and they needed all the supplies they could safely carry.

Opening a can of peaches, he set it on the table. "Dig in," he said, handing her one of the forks and taking the other for himself.

The impending walk on both their minds, they ate the fruit quickly and without much conversation. "You're sure you'll be able to walk today?" Chloe asked, nodding toward his leg with a frown.

"I'm sure I have no choice," he answered with a shrug. "The longer we wait here, the more chance both of us have of being hurt again or coming down with infections from the injuries we've already sustained."

She sighed almost imperceptibly, but nodded with characteristic acceptance of logic. "I would like to wash up before we start out."

"So would I. Tell you what, why don't I go first just to make sure it's all clear outside. I won't be long. While I'm gone, see if you can figure out a way to carry cans of fruit that won't weigh either of us down too badly."

"I'll see what I can find. But are you sure you don't want me to walk out with you? I'm afraid you're going to fall again."

He leaned on the heavy stick, demonstrating how sturdy it was. "I'll be fine. I'm able to keep most of my weight off the bad leg."

"Just be careful," she warned him.

"I will."

Trying to minimize his limp for her sake, he made his way to the door and opened it, wincing at the shrill creak of rusty hinges. Someone needed to—

The sight of the scruffy man standing on the other side of the door, holding a shotgun leveled directly at him, made Donovan forget all about the creaky hinges.

Chapter Nine

"What the hell are you doing in my cabin?" the armed man, whom Donovan judged to be in his late fifties, demanded in a harsh voice.

Chloe's gasp from behind Donovan indicated that she had seen the gun. He motioned with his left hand for her to be calm, even as he held the man's gaze with his own.

"I'm sorry for trespassing on your property," he said, keeping his tone placating. "We got lost in the forest and we—"

His faded blue eyes glittering in a weathered, whiskery face, the armed man cut in, "Who do you work for? IRS? CIA?"

Donovan recognized that there would be no negotiating with this guy. He shook his head. "You've got it all wrong. We're on the run. See those cuffs on your table?"

The other man looked away just long enough to spot the handcuffs. Still pointed directly at Donovan's heart, the shotgun never wavered.

Without waiting for a response, Donovan added, "I took those off last night. The feds are out there looking for us now. They hear a gunshot, they'll come down on this place before you can blink twice."

The other man frowned, then made a motion with the gun. "Get out. And then keep going."

"We're going," Donovan said, motioning for Chloe to join him. He wanted to get her out of here before the guy changed his mind about sending them away.

"But my friend is hurt," Chloe protested, looking at the angry man in disbelief. "His leg could be broken. And we don't know which direction to go for help. Couldn't you at least—"

The shotgun leveled directly at Donovan's chest again. "Out," its owner growled. "I ain't giving you another warning."

"We're going," Donovan assured him again, leaning on the stick as he took a careful step forward.

"And leave that here! That's my good stick."

Donovan quickly set the stick aside, then held up both hands to show that they were empty. "No problem. My friend here will help me, won't you, Chloe?"

She still seemed to find it impossible to believe that this man wasn't going to offer them assistance. "But couldn't we at least—"

His eyes on that steady shotgun, Donovan spoke sharply this time. "*Now,* Chloe."

Subsiding into a bewildered silence, she moved beside him and offered him her shoulder for support.

Donovan made sure to exaggerate his limp as they made their way slowly out the door—not that he had to play it up much, since his leg really did hurt like the devil. He wanted to appear as non-threatening as possible to the other man.

The scruffy man watched them suspiciously, staying on guard against any sudden moves. When they were outside, he stepped into his doorway as if to prevent them from going back inside. "Don't come back here," he warned. "You won't be leaving again if you do."

"You won't see us again," Donovan replied.

The door slammed shut. Then immediately opened again. "Get moving!" he shouted. "And stay off my road. I'll be watching it. You know what will happen if I find you again."

"We're leaving." Donovan nudged Chloe toward the woods. "And don't worry, we never saw you."

They made their way as swiftly as possible into the shelter of the trees. Donovan's back itched with the awareness that there was a shotgun aimed right at the center of it.

He heaved a slight sigh of relief when they reached the tree line and slipped into it, letting themselves be swallowed by the shadows. Only then did they hear the crash of the cabin door closing again.

Releasing his grip on Chloe's shoulder, Donovan reached out to prop himself with one hand against the trunk of a large tree, needing a moment to get his equilibrium. He might have seemed calm, but his heart was pounding like a jackhammer against his ribs. He'd been scared that he would do or say something wrong and put Chloe in further jeopardy.

Realizing that Chloe was frowning at him in heavy silence, he lifted his eyebrows at her. "What?"

"You could have at least tried to reason with him."

"I could have," he agreed equably. "But I really wasn't in the mood to get shot today."

"You really think he would have shot us? Even if we had taken the time to make him understand that we—?"

"Chloe," he interrupted her gently. "Do you know what that guy is probably doing right this minute?"

She blinked a minute, then shook her head. "No."

"He's probably searching every inch of that cabin for the listening devices he's certain we've placed there. He's convinced himself by now that I was lying to him, that we're really government agents who were spying on his activities. He doesn't believe I have a broken leg, or that we have no idea where we are. The only reason he didn't shoot us is because he was afraid the sound of shots would make our army of jackbooted partners rush in to rescue us. If we'd waited much longer, he would have taken the chance and shot us, anyway."

"But—"

"He's not sane, Chloe. He's scared and confused and paranoid. There was no chance of negotiating with him without putting both our lives at risk. And besides, there's not that much he could have done to help us, anyway."

Biting her lip, she looked back toward the cabin. "I was just surprised that you cooperated so easily with him."

"What would you have had me do? Tell him he had no right to throw us out of his own cabin? If I *had* tried to fight him, and by some miracle I had overpowered him without getting shot, would you have had me beat him up for protecting his few belongings?"

She sighed. "Not when you put it that way."

"If you'd ever stumbled into a bear's den, you'd know how dangerous it is to surprise a wild creature in its lair. That's pretty much what we just did."

"I take it you've stumbled into a bear's den before?"

"Yeah." He glanced back toward the cabin, and pushed away from the tree. "And we'd better get moving before this particular bear decides to come out and make sure we're gone."

She hurried to support him. "I didn't see a car anywhere around the cabin when we left. How do you suppose he got there?"

"He could have been on foot, maybe camping out all night. He obviously hadn't been to the cabin in a while, so maybe he has other hidey holes and switches around between them—to make himself harder to find, of course. If he has a vehicle of some sort, it's probably an old junker to haul a few supplies in."

"Maybe we could find it. You could hot-wire it, and we could, well, borrow it to get to safety and then make sure he gets it back when we're rescued. Or return an even nicer one, maybe, to compensate him for the inconvenience."

Donovan cocked an eyebrow at her without pausing in his walking. "What makes you think I know how to hot-wire a car?"

She responded with a delicate snort. "Anyone who knows how to open handcuffs with a hairpin would surely know how to hot-wire a car. You do, don't you?"

"Yes," he answered with a shrug. "But it doesn't matter. Even if he's got a vehicle, I'm sure he has it hidden so well that he would find us again before we came across it. It's not worth it, Chloe. We'd be better off walking until we find someone more willing to help us."

"*If* we find anyone willing to help us."

"We will," he assured her. "Just remember what you promised me last night. Don't give up."

He watched her draw her shoulders straighter, her chin rising to a stubborn tilt. "I'm not giving up. I can keep going if you can."

"Good. See that big, forked branch over there? It looks to be about the size I need for a walking stick. Want to fetch it for me?"

Stepping carefully over rocks and pinecones, Chloe made her way to the stick and then returned it to him. As he'd hoped, it made a pretty decent crutch.

"It doesn't look exactly comfortable," Chloe commented, eyeing him doubtfully as he supported his weight on the sturdy branch.

He shrugged. "It's okay."

"You've had worse, right?"

He had to smile a little at her ironic tone. "Right."

Muttering beneath her breath, she fell into pace with his slow but steady steps. He wasn't sure what she said, but it sounded like, "Ten steps at a time."

Hell of a way to start the new day, he thought again. But at least it had stopped raining. For now.

The befuddled man with the shotgun didn't have to worry about finding them on "his" road, Chloe thought later. She and Donovan had been slowly making their way for hours, and had yet to come across anything that actually resembled a road.

Donovan's theory was that the hermit hid his vehicle some distance from the cabin and hiked the rest of the way, either to avoid leading anyone to the place or because the terrain directly around the cabin was too rough to traverse in whatever vehicle he possessed. Apparently, he and Chloe had blundered off in the wrong direction when they'd made their hasty exit from the cabin.

For all he knew, they could be walking deeper into the forest rather than out of it.

"What about supplies? How does he get them to his cabin? There certainly wasn't enough there for him to survive on for more than a day or two." Chloe tried to keep one eye on their path and the other on Donovan as she spoke. She worried about him falling again, or somehow re-injuring his leg. It was insane that he was attempting this walk with a broken bone, but it wasn't as if they really had any other choice, either.

"He probably stashes supplies nearby. Cases of canned food and bottled water, that sort of thing."

Chloe thought of the way Donovan had spoken of the armed man with something close to compassion. "He really is a strange, sad man, isn't he?"

"Yeah. One of those unfortunate cases that slipped through the cracks of the veterans' system."

"You think he's a veteran?"

"You didn't notice the fatigue jacket or the boots?"

"All I saw was the gun," she admitted a bit sheepishly.

He nodded. "I focused fairly intently on that shot-gun, myself."

He paused, leaning heavily on his improvised crutch, and studied the area ahead. Stopping beside him, Chloe, too, looked forward. The sight was enough to make her gulp. They'd hit rough patches before during the hours they'd spent in this forest, but this time they'd reached a particularly difficult area.

Erosion from an ancient, fast-flowing river had carved a deep furrow into the rocky ground. Still wet from the heavy rains yesterday, the ground around the ravine looked slippery and treacherous. Heavy under-brush lined the narrow clearing they'd been follow-ing, and a steep limestone bluff rose on their right, preventing them from going that direction without climbing. Behind them, of course, was a crazy man with a shotgun—and possibly three armed kidnap-pers.

She felt her shoulders sag. She wasn't giving up, she assured herself. But she was so tired of having one obstacle after another thrown their way. It felt sometimes as if the whole universe was conspiring against them—and yet they'd survived it so far, she reminded herself. Battered, but unbroken. At least for now.

"I don't know about you, but I'm ready for a break," Donovan said, making her wonder if he found the scene ahead as daunting as she did.

"Definitely," she agreed.

They found a mossy patch of ground in the shade of a twisted old hickory tree. Chloe helped Donovan lower himself to sit, then sat beside him.

It felt good to be off her feet again. It was warmer today than it had been, the sun shining straight down through the holes in the clouds that still covered most of the sky. She wouldn't have preferred the rains of yesterday, but she hoped it didn't get too hot as the afternoon wore on.

Bolstering her courage, she decided to examine her feet. She noted in resignation that her socks were now torn on both sides. Several new scrapes decorated her feet, but she supposed she'd grown accustomed to the constant, nagging throbbing. It was like a dull toothache—unpleasant, relentless, but tolerable for now.

"How are your feet?" Donovan asked, just as she noticed an area of exposed skin on the ball of her right foot that was beginning to look particularly inflamed and nasty.

Infection, she thought, turning the foot so he couldn't see it as she replied, "They're okay. How's your leg?"

"Hardly bothers me at all."

They were both lying, of course, and they both knew it. But neither felt the need to examine those lies at the moment.

Sitting side by side, their legs stretched in front of them, they sat in silence for a while, resting and contemplating their situation.

Chloe was the one who broke the silence, as usual. "Donovan?"

"Mm?"

"What time do you think it is?"

It didn't surprise her when he glanced up at the sky and answered matter-of-factly, "Around two o'clock. Maybe two-thirty."

She touched her empty stomach. "Too bad we don't have a can of fruit cocktail lying around, isn't it?"

"Mm. Want to try an acorn?"

"Thanks, but I'll hold out for a nice, fresh salad when we get rescued. With lots of crunchy veggies and breadsticks on the side."

He grunted. "You can have the rabbit food. I want meat. Red. Medium-rare. Maybe a baked potato with some butter and sour cream."

"And what would you have for dessert? Personally, I'd like a bowl of sherbet. Pineapple—maybe orange."

"Coconut pie topped with a couple inches of meringue," Donovan countered without even stopping to think about it.

"Your favorite from the diner," she remembered with a smile.

It was obvious that he didn't like to be reminded of the diner where they had been taken. He nodded shortly, his expression grim.

She hurried to keep the conversation moving. "Did your mother make pies like that?"

"My mother didn't do much baking. She sometimes made fried pies for a treat. They were good—especially peach."

He'd mentioned the first day they met that he had no family. "When did you lose her?" she asked quietly.

"I was eleven. She died of an infection that set in after a relatively minor surgery."

Neither his voice nor his expression had changed when he answered her question. She took a chance and asked another. "And your father?"

"Took off when I was six. I never saw him again, and my mother never remarried."

"No brothers or sisters?"

"No."

She bit her lip, then asked, "Who raised you after your mother died?"

"Assorted distant relatives. By the time I was fourteen, I was pretty much on my own."

She remembered his description of himself as a "wild, redneck kid." No wonder he'd been wild.

Her heart went out to the lonely little boy he must have been. And she couldn't help admiring the capable, influential man he had become.

Apparently deciding he'd talked enough about his past, Donovan changed the subject. "I figure we were grabbed about forty-three, maybe forty-four hours ago. Wonder how much progress Bryan's made in tracking us down?"

"He wouldn't have already paid a ransom, would he? Not without proof that we're safe?"

"No." He spoke confidently. "He wouldn't do that unless he knew without doubt that he could grab them while they were trying to collect."

"Do you think the kidnappers are still looking for us?"

"It's a good bet that they are. We're their only bargaining chip. I'm sure they'll try bluffing, try to convince Bryan that they have us and that he'd better pay up quickly or they'll kill us. But Bryan isn't easy to fool. They'll want to find us before we get to a phone. They'd have been watching for news that we've been rescued. Since there has been no such report, they'll likely figure out the truth—that we're still wandering in the forest. They know how treacherous the terrain can be, and it was dark when we headed out. They might even figure we've fallen off a bluff, or have been hurt in some other way."

She touched one of the slats that made up the leg splint they had rigged for him. "They wouldn't be entirely wrong—but I doubt that they could imagine how far we've walked, considering everything."

He let that comment go without answer, which worried her a little. Maybe he thought the kidnappers were closer on their trail than Chloe realized. She spoke quickly to push that worrisome thought out of her mind. "Do you think Bryan has any idea who took us, or why?"

"I wouldn't be surprised if he's coming close to answers, if he hasn't already figured them out. Those last-minute distractions were a foolish mistake on Childers's part. He might as well have given notice that he was trying to detain Bryan in New York for as long as possible."

"If Bryan's reasoned that much out, will he confront Childers?"

"Oh, yeah. If he can find him. And if he does, I'd hate to be in Childers's shoes," Donovan replied with grim satisfaction.

"Then maybe Bryan has tracked us to that cabin. And if he's gotten that far, maybe he knows we're out here. Maybe he's got search-and-rescue teams looking for us even now."

Donovan made an obvious effort not to dampen her optimism. "Maybe so."

She looked up. A few faint trails of high-flying airplanes traced across the spring-blue sky as scattered clouds floated lazily overhead. But she'd seen no small planes or helicopters or anything that implied a search in progress. Whatever Bryan was doing on his end, it was still up to her and Donovan to make as much headway as possible on their own.

She turned to face him, scooting down to his injured leg. "I want to check these bindings."

Keeping her touch as gentle as possible, she adjusted the wooden slats they had used for splint material and made sure the stretchy T-shirt fabric was holding them in place as snugly as possible. She had no idea whether this contraption they'd rigged was protecting the bone from further damage, but she didn't know what else they could do under the circumstances.

She looked up at him. He had bent his head to watch what she was doing, so their faces were very close together now.

"Look like it's going to hold?" he asked without pulling back.

"I hope so. I just don't know if it's doing any good," she admitted.

He shrugged. "It's the best we can do for the moment."

"That's pretty much what I've concluded. Are you in much pain? And tell me the truth, don't be all macho and brush me off."

"It hurts," he answered candidly. "Sometimes more than other times. Just like you must hurt with every step you take. But since the only way we're getting out of here is to keep walking, it does no good to concentrate on the pain."

"I suppose you've hiked on a broken leg before?"

His mouth quirked into that semi-smile that she was finding more appealing all the time. "Something like that."

"I thought so. I just hope your leg holds out until we get ourselves rescued."

Suddenly aware of how close they were sitting, she

told herself she should move away. Their gazes were locked, their mouths only inches apart. She glanced downward, noting that his mouth wasn't curved into a smile now—but it still looked entirely too appealing.

She couldn't help wondering if Donovan Chance kissed as competently and skillfully as he seemed to do everything else.

"We'd better find out."

His words made her blink. Surely he didn't mean…

"We'd better get going," he added, as if he wasn't quite sure she'd heard him.

She must have looked like an idiot, scrambling to her feet with her cheeks on fire, but she needed a little distance from him just then. She barely gave him time to struggle to his feet before she pressed on, making her way very carefully across the treacherous ground—and feeling as though she had just missed stepping onto a path that could prove every bit as dangerous as this one.

They sat in another dark cave, this one a mere indentation in a limestone wall. Donovan's outstretched legs barely fit inside; had they been an inch longer they'd have been sticking out. There wasn't room for either of them to stand up, but it provided a cozy shelter in which to rest for the night.

The sun had been setting when Donovan spotted the cave, and it had been he who'd suggested they stop here for the night. It hadn't been too soon to call it a day as far as Chloe was concerned.

As the hours had worn on, the terrain had become even more perilous. Their progress had been painfully slow and tedious as they had made their way around heavy brush, large boulders, fallen trees, gaping holes and slippery patches of mud left from yesterday's heavy rains. There had been times when it had seemed they were making no headway, when it would have been easier to simply sit down and cry.

She'd kept going because she had no choice—but she had stopped counting her steps. They'd moved at such a snail's pace that it had been too depressing to count that slowly.

"*How* long was that little girl lost in the forest?" she asked after she and Donovan had been resting in the cave for a while in silence.

He must have sensed that she was growing discouraged. "A few days. I can't remember, exactly. It happens often, actually. Hikers are always getting lost, falling off bluffs and whatever, and it sometimes takes days to find them, even with whole teams of searchers."

"It just seems like we would have seen some sign of civilization by now. Something besides that poor, strange man's cabin."

"If we're where I think we are, this is a million-acre forest. Federally protected wilderness, no development encouraged. We're bound to come across someone before too much longer, but it's not so strange that we've been able to wander around for two days without finding our way out."

"What if we're wandering in circles? Maybe heading away from people instead of toward them."

"We're not traveling in circles. Zigzagging a bit, but not circles."

"You're sure?"

"Positive."

Either he really was certain—or he lied as well as he did everything else.

"I'm not giving up," she said wearily.

"I know you're not. But I can't blame you for being discouraged. You're exhausted."

"You must be, too."

"I'm tired, but I slept well last night."

So had she, actually. She'd roused only a couple of times to strange sounds, and both times she'd drifted straight back into sleep, safe and warm in Donovan's arms.

Her growing attachment to him—dependence upon him?—was beginning to worry her. She'd been fascinated by him since the moment she'd met him, but it seemed to be developing into something more than that. Was it only proximity? Only the fact that her safety—perhaps her very life—depended on him now?

Or was it more than that?

She'd long since given up on finding a real hero— a true soul mate. The kind of man she'd fantasized about meeting when she'd been younger and more idealistic. She'd convinced herself that she was willing to settle for a compatible partner—someone she liked very much, with whom she had a great deal in common. Someone like Bryan.

She was beginning to understand how close she was coming to making a huge mistake.

"You're being very quiet all of a sudden," Donovan murmured. "Blaming me for getting you into this mess?"

"I'm trusting you to get me out of it," she replied more lightly than she felt.

"I hope I can justify your faith in me."

"Something tells me you will."

Though it was too dark to see his face clearly, she sensed his frown. "I'll do my best. But, Chloe—I've made mistakes in the past. And people have been hurt because of them."

"We've all unintentionally hurt people."

Shaking his head, he muttered, "That's not what I meant."

She laid a hand on his arm, feeling the tenseness of his muscles. "I know you've led a...colorful past. And I won't deny I'm curious, which is only natural considering how much time we've spent together. But whatever mistakes you've made, I can't imagine anyone more capable or resourceful or tenacious than you've been since those men grabbed us."

She couldn't see his face in the darkness, but he covered her hand with his and spoke quietly, "I'll get you out of this, Chloe."

"We'll get each other out," she replied, leaning her head against his shoulder. "We just need some rest tonight. Tomorrow we'll find civilization."

"And then you can have that salad you've been fantasizing about."

In response to the mention of food, her stomach growled softly. "Actually, that red meat you mentioned is starting to sound pretty good."

"Then I'll buy you a steak as soon as we find a restaurant," he promised rashly. "With a salad on the side. Followed by sherbet—pineapple or orange, right?"

"You're starting to know me well," she teased.

When he spoke again, his mouth was very close to her ear. "Maybe I am."

All she had to do was turn her head and their lips

would touch. Her curiosity about kissing him would finally be satisfied.

Only a few days ago, Chloe wouldn't have had the courage to move. But the last forty-eight hours had changed her. She had learned to take advantage of every opportunity that presented itself to her.

She turned her head.

Chapter Ten

Chloe's lips brushed Donovan's jaw, just as they had the night before when she'd given him that impulsive good-night kiss. And then she adjusted her aim so that their lips met.

For only one tantalizing moment he responded. His lips moved against hers, warm and firm and skilled. It was wonderful—but unsatisfying. She wanted more.

She could almost feel his urge to take her into his arms and deepen the embrace. A short, hard tremor seemed to course through him at the same time a jolt of pleasure shook her—and then, abruptly, he drew away.

"I'll consider that a very nice thank you," he said, and though he tried to speak lightly, his voice was rough-edged.

She moistened her lips, which still tingled in reaction to that brief contact and ached with a hunger for more. "Donovan—"

"Bryan will be glad to see you if—when—we do find our way back," he added, drawing even farther away from her physically so that they were barely touching now. "Your sister, too, of course. I just hope she doesn't blame all this on Bryan, since she seemed so eager to find fault with him, anyway."

He'd used Bryan's name like a shield—and she realized now it wasn't the first time he had done so.

Leaning back against the cool rock wall, she told herself she shouldn't take his withdrawal as a personal rejection. Under the circumstances, he was being prudent to hold back. After all, he worked for the man with whom she'd been discussing marriage. And he probably wondered—as she did—if their emotions were being heightened by the drama of their situation. If there was a natural tendency to turn to each other because they had no one else to turn to.

"Grace won't blame Bryan for this," she said, deciding to follow his example. "At least…I don't think she will," she added a bit less confidently.

"If she does, she'll just have to get over it. This wasn't Bryan's fault."

"I've already assured you that I know that. And Grace will understand once she hears all the facts."

Donovan grunted. "Yeah. Then she'll probably blame *me*."

"She'll blame the people who are responsible. Just as I do. And you aren't one of them."

After a short pause, Donovan asked, "You and your sister are very close, aren't you?"

"Of course. We're twins. And best friends. I know your first impression of her wasn't good, but she's really a lot of fun. She's big-hearted and generous and has a great sense of humor.''

''And a temper.''

''And a temper,'' Chloe agreed wryly.

''Did she get it all? Or have you been known to blow your top occasionally?''

''Oh, I have a temper. It just takes longer to set mine off than it does Grace's.''

There was another pause, and then Donovan spoke again. ''Do you think your sister will accept your decision to marry Bryan? It would be difficult for you if your twin couldn't get along with your husband.''

He'd spoken without any particular emotion, but the word *husband* seemed to reverberate for a moment in the shallow cave.

Chloe swallowed, then replied, ''I've told you repeatedly, Donovan, I have not agreed to marry Bryan.''

''He's asked you, hasn't he?''

''He suggested it might be an advantageous arrangement for both of us,'' she replied carefully. ''I told him I would consider his proposition.''

''You decided to accept, didn't you? You wouldn't have agreed to spend this week with him if you hadn't pretty well made up your mind already.''

He *was* getting to know her well. And, truth was, she had almost made up her mind to marry Bryan when she'd agreed to join him here. But things had changed since then.

Was Donovan trying in his not-so-subtle way to find out her true feelings for Bryan? Was he interested only as Bryan's friend—or for more personal reasons?

She decided to answer him candidly. ''I had almost convinced myself that I would never have a better offer. Bryan is an extraordinary man and I've grown quite fond of him during the past few weeks. I want a family—children—and I'm not getting any younger. I thought I would be foolish not to at least give his flattering offer careful consideration. But that was before—''

''Before?''

Before I met you. She hadn't grown quite brave enough to let those words escape.

''Before I decided that my sister was right about one thing,'' she answered instead. ''I don't want to marry anyone because it seems like the logical and practical thing to do at the time. I want it to mean more than that.''

''You, uh, really shouldn't be making *any* decisions under these circumstances,'' Donovan said somewhat awkwardly. ''You're exhausted and scared, and you can't think clearly like that. Things that you feel out here—well, you can't trust that they're real.''

So Donovan *was* worried that their emotions were being influenced by their situation. Maybe he was warning himself as much as her. And while she acknowledged the validity of his concerns, she didn't really believe she was letting herself be overly influenced by circumstances.

True, the past forty-eight hours had thrown them together so that they'd had no choice but to get to know each other, to lean on each other and depend on each other. But there had to be more to it than that.

What she was starting to feel for Donovan was too powerful to be mere infatuation, too compelling to be simple attraction. She had never been the sort of woman who fell in love easily—and she wasn't quite ready yet to say she was in love with Donovan—but it was more than circumstantial.

Because she wasn't at all sure of his feelings for *her,* she said simply, "I'm not making any big decisions tonight."

That seemed to satisfy him—at least enough that he let the subject drop. "You'd better get some sleep. We'll start early in the morning."

An outcropping of rock jutted from the cave wall beside her. Using her arm for a pillow, she laid her head on it and closed her eyes while Donovan leaned against the opposite wall. The only sound in the cave came from the wildlife outside.

They wouldn't be nestling together tonight. Donovan had deliberately withdrawn from her since he'd brought up Bryan's name.

He was absolutely right to do so, of course, she reflected as she pretended to sleep. As he'd said, this was no time to make important decisions. Or to take rash actions. After that, she needed to have a long talk with Bryan. And after that...

She couldn't say now whether she and Donovan would ever spend time together after they were rescued. But she suspected that it wouldn't be her decision if they did not.

Grace had worried about her being hurt during this vacation. Chloe had wondered if there was a chance she could fall in love this week.

She spent a long time reflecting on the ironic aspects of those uncanny predictions. It gave her something to do besides think about how very close Donovan sat to her—and how nice it would have felt to be lying in his arms rather than against a cold, hard rock.

* * *

A wireless telephone in his hand, Bryan Falcon sat in the den of his Ozarks vacation home and gazed somberly at the woman sleeping restlessly on the couch across the room. He'd draped an afghan over her earlier and she had stirred, but, to his relief, she hadn't awakened. He'd needed a break from her pacing and questioning.

He'd tried to talk her into taking one of the bedrooms for the night, but she'd refused. She wouldn't sleep, she had vowed, until Donovan and Chloe were safe.

She'd lasted until nearly 2:00 a.m. before sleep had claimed her. Bryan couldn't remember the last time he'd slept, but he couldn't rest yet.

She looked so much like Chloe, he thought, studying Grace's face in the soft glow of the only lamp he'd left on in the room. And yet they were so different. When he was with Chloe, he always felt comfortable. Peaceful.

Peaceful was not the first word that came to mind when he thought of Grace. Neither was *comfortable*. He felt as though there were several large strips of his skin missing after spending the past several hours with her. She most definitely blamed him for the danger her sister was in now.

He'd held on to his patience only because he understood how greatly she had suffered today as the hours had crept by with no word of Chloe. He'd talked her out of calling her parents, but there'd been no way he could make her stay home and leave everything to him. She had insisted on joining him here, on knowing every detail of what he was doing to find Chloe.

There had been no further ransom calls, and that was starting to make him even more nervous.

The kidnappers should be pushing him, demanding that he hand over the money immediately. Even if— and he had to swallow at the thought—even if Chloe and Donovan were dead, the kidnappers should be bluffing, working to convince Bryan that they were unharmed and would stay that way if he paid the ransom.

But something was very wrong on that other end. He knew it…and so did Grace.

Rubbing his forehead, he wondered how he could live with himself if anything had happened to Chloe because of him. And losing Donovan was something he couldn't even think about right now.

Grace shifted on the couch, opened her eyes, then sat straight upright. "How long have I been asleep?"

"A little over an hour."

She looked at the phone in his hand. "Have you…?"

"There's been no word yet. I had the phone set to vibrate so it wouldn't startle you if it rang."

She shoved the afghan away. "What time is it?"

"Just after 3:00 a.m. Are you sure you won't lie down upstairs for awhile? I promise I'll wake you if I hear anything at all."

Wearing the stubborn look he'd come to expect from her, she shook her head. "I couldn't sleep in that room with Chloe's things all around me."

"You could take one of the other rooms."

"I don't want to sleep. I want to find my sister."

"We're doing everything we can, Grace."

"Then do more."

"I know it looks as though I'm not doing enough,

but believe me, I am. I'm just trying to keep it quiet. I want to keep the media away from this as long as possible. It hasn't been easy doing so this long, and we won't be able to hide it much longer, but if the press gets wind of what's happened, we'll have a circus on our hands. That could be dangerous for Chloe and Donovan.''

He'd explained that to her before, but he figured it was worth reiterating. Grace had never experienced the press in full feeding frenzy. He had.

She started to say something else, but was interrupted when Jason Colby walked into the room, a look of grim satisfaction on his face.

Bryan jumped to his feet. Across the room, Grace did the same.

''I've got news,'' Jason announced.

As if she needed reassurance—even if it came from him—Grace moved closer to Bryan. ''Tell us,'' she said, her voice strained. ''Where is my sister?''

With Chloe cradled in his arms, Donovan watched the gray light of another cloudy dawn creep slowly into the shallow cave. The temperature had dropped during the night, and he'd sensed Chloe shivering in her sleep.

He still had the old vet's matches in his pocket, and he had considered building a small fire. But since the cave wasn't ventilated and he was more likely to asphyxiate them than warm them, he'd turned to the only other source of warmth he'd had to offer—body heat.

Chloe hadn't roused when he'd pulled her into his arms, which only proved the extent of her exhaustion.

He decided the cool nights were much preferable

to what they'd have been suffering if they'd been stranded in the forest in August rather than April. Dangerous heat, burning sun, higher risk of dehydration, more problems with insects and snakes...he supposed if they had to be lost in the woods this was the best time for it to happen. The biggest problem with spring was the threat of severe weather—and he'd been hearing thunder rolling in the distance for about an hour now.

Though Chloe still shivered occasionally, her face felt warm when he laid the back of his hand against her cheek. He hoped she wasn't getting sick, though he wouldn't be surprised if she was.

He honestly didn't know how she kept going. Little sleep, less food, only occasional sips of water from the stream, the bottoms of her feet shredded. He was hardly in top shape, himself, but he'd had more experience with this sort of thing—from boot camp to Saudi Arabia and assorted other demanding locales.

As he'd thought several times before, Chloe was definitely tougher than she looked.

He could still almost taste her lips on his. Could still feel their texture, their warmth, their softness. And it took very little stretch of his imagination to fantasize about taking the kiss further and making love with her—in a bed or here in this wannabe cave. Those fantasies had kept him awake all night.

Being neither stupid nor oblivious, he was well aware that Chloe had developed an attraction for him. As mutual as those feelings might be, he was making a massive effort not to let them get out of hand.

He had seen his share of what he'd always thought of as ''battle-zone romances''—relationships that developed rapidly under intense conditions, then fizzled just as swiftly when life returned to normal. He wouldn't risk anything of that sort with Chloe.

For another thing, he would be betraying Bryan—something he'd long ago vowed never to do.

Even if Chloe was starting to have doubts about her future with Bryan, Donovan had no intention of taking advantage of those misgivings. Despite her repeated assertions that she didn't blame Bryan for this situation, he wasn't sure that she wasn't secretly harboring some resentment. The very natural anger she surely felt had to find an outlet. After the kidnappers themselves, she probably directed at least part of it toward Bryan.

Considering Bryan's renowned charm, Donovan didn't think it would take his friend long to get past that repressed resentment once Chloe was safely back with him.

But it wasn't just loyalty alone that was making Donovan hold Chloe at emotional arm's length, though that would have been enough in itself. There was also the niggling suspicion that his own emotions were being unduly influenced by their circumstances. It seemed uncharacteristic of him, but how else could he explain his growing fascination with her?

Sure, she was pretty. And intelligent. Resilient. And brave. Everything he admired most in a woman. But it seemed like more than that this time.

He couldn't stop thinking about her. Couldn't stop watching her. Couldn't help wanting to take care of her, even though she'd proven quite capable of taking care of herself. He'd never been particularly susceptible to battle-zone romance, but he supposed there was a first time for everything.

Since Chloe was going to be a significant part of

his life if Bryan convinced her to marry him—and Bryan's powers of persuasion were legendary—Donovan didn't want to do anything that would create more awkwardness between them than would already exist now. Any lingering feelings he had for her when this was over—well, he would deal with them then.

In the meantime, he would keep things between them friendly, cordial, as pleasant as possible under the circumstances. But not too personal. He had to keep emotion out of it, and rely on logic instead.

She stirred against him, the movement brushing her soft breasts against his chest. And then she opened her eyes and gave him a sleepy smile. "Is it morning already?"

He had to clear his throat hard before he could speak. "Yeah."

Keeping his emotions under control for however long it took to get them out of this forest wasn't going to be at all easy. It was going to be a continuous battle between logic and emotion—and, to his surprise, he couldn't be certain of which would eventually win out.

Definitely a new experience for him.

They had planned to start walking at first light. It was a little after that time when they finally made their way out of the cave, tried to stretch out the stiffness and soreness from their cramped sleeping quarters, and then agreed which direction to head in first.

Thinking she looked pale, Donovan asked Chloe several times if she wanted to wait a while longer before getting started, but she assured him she was ready. The sky was growing darker by the moment, which indicated another impending rainstorm. They needed to make as much progress as possible before it began, she pointed out.

She made it less than three yards before she collapsed.

Donovan caught her just before she hit the ground. The impact knocked the makeshift crutch from his hand, forcing him to stagger, his weight coming down on his injured leg. A sharp hiss escaped between his teeth, and they fell together, but somehow he managed to cushion their landing.

Pushing the awareness of his own pain to the back of his mind, he struggled to sit up. Once he'd accomplished that feat, he bent over Chloe, who lay on her back beside him, her breath escaping in soft moans. "Chloe?"

Her eyelids fluttered. Her voice was very weak. "I—I'm sorry. I think I...fainted."

He touched her cheek. Her face felt hotter now than it had before. Her eyes were glazed and there were dark circles beneath them, in stark contrast to her face, which was pale except for two vivid patches of red on her cheeks.

"You haven't eaten," he murmured, stroking a damp strand of hair away from her face. "And you have a slight fever."

"Slight" was an understatement, of course. She was burning up. But he saw no need to go into technicalities at the moment. "I'll get you some water. Wait here."

"I can walk," she said, but she didn't move.

"Just lie still. I'll be right back."

He groped for his crutch, then used both hands to drag himself upright with it. The stream was nearby, but he had nothing to carry water in. The knife and matches he'd filched from the cabin were still in his pocket, but they did him no good at the moment. He settled for tossing the crutch aside and cupping his hands.

His right foot dragging behind him, he made his way painfully back to Chloe's side. Kneeling beside her sent fiery spears of pain stabbing through his leg; he ignored them as he held his hands to her lips. Water trickled down her chin, but he was satisfied that she drank a little. He fervently hoped it wasn't stream water making her sick—but he suspected the infection in her feet was spreading.

Just the thought of spreading infection made his heart beat faster in fear. He couldn't help remembering that an infection had killed his mother. He had to push those old memories ruthlessly aside to keep his hands steady for Chloe.

When his hands were empty again, he made his way slowly back to the stream, where he removed one of the strips of cloth from his splint and soaked it in the cold water. And then, setting his teeth against the pain, he returned to her.

She was trying to rouse herself, having worked her way up to one elbow. Donovan pressed a hand gently against her shoulder. "Lie back down. You'll get dizzy again."

"I can walk."

"Chloe. Lie down." He laid the cool fabric against her face when she reluctantly complied. "It's still very early. We've got time for you to recuperate awhile before we start moving again."

She closed her eyes, looking suddenly frail and vulnerable. But her chin was firm when she murmured, "I'm not giving up."

An odd pang shot through his chest. His reply was gruff. "I know you aren't. You never give up, do you, General?"

She didn't smile at the nickname as she had the last time he'd teased her with it. Instead, she whispered, "Sometimes I do."

He stroked the cloth against her fever-reddened cheeks. "Not this time."

"No. Not this time." Drawing a deep breath, she opened her eyes again. "I'm sorry. I keep holding us up."

"Hey, I'm the one with the gimpy leg, remember? I'm hardly moving at top speed these days."

She tried to laugh, a rather pathetic attempt. "We're both in pretty sorry shape, aren't we?"

"I won't give up if you won't."

She reached up to push the cool cloth away from her face. "Then let's get moving, shall we?"

He tried to talk her into resting a little longer, but she was determined to prove that she could keep walking if he could. She swayed just a bit when he helped her to her feet, but she quickly steadied herself, spreading her feet and squaring her shoulders as she pushed her hair out of her face and started walking.

He followed close at her heels, ready to catch her if she staggered again.

Damn, but it was getting harder every minute to keep himself from falling for her. It had to be circumstantial, he assured himself. His feelings would pass when they returned to their own world.

But his feelings sure as hell felt real now.

To Chloe's chagrin, they hadn't walked very far before her vision started to blur again. Her ears buzzed and perspiration beaded above her lip. She tried to clench her teeth and forge on, but everything began to go gray around her. She knew she had to stop before she passed out again. "Donovan?"

He put a hand beneath her elbow. "Dizzy?"

"A little. You think we could rest for a minute?"

"As long as you need. Sit down. Put your head between your legs."

She followed his instructions, and was relieved when the world finally stopped spinning. "I'm sorry. I—"

"Would you stop apologizing? I need a rest, too. My leg hurts like hell."

That brought her head back up. "Do you think you've re-injured it? Is there anything I can do?"

He placed a hand on her shoulder. "You worry about your health and I'll worry about mine, okay?"

Though the words were brusque, his gentle tone belied them. She knew full well that he was more worried about her than he was about himself. "Right," she answered lightly. "I'll be completely selfish. Doesn't matter to me if your leg falls right off."

"That's the spirit," he replied with a hint of a smile.

Her own smile faded as another wave of weakness coursed through her. She put her head down again.

Donovan's hand tightened on her shoulder. "Want me to get you some water?"

"No, thank you. Maybe I'll just lie down for a few minutes."

He urged her to lie with her head on his left thigh rather than on the rocky ground. She felt his fingers in her hair as he brushed it away from her fever-dampened face.

"It seems warmer today," she murmured, her eyes closed, her head pillowed comfortably on his firm thigh.

"Maybe a little. I'm afraid we're facing another thunderstorm. Those clouds don't look promising."

She spoke without opening her eyes. "I've been hearing a lot of thunder. Seems like it's getting closer. How far do you think we've walked since we left the cave?"

He hesitated a moment, then said, "Maybe a mile. A mile and a half at the most."

She frowned. "That's all? But we've been walking for hours."

"A couple of hours. We just haven't been moving very quickly."

"Have you seen any signs of civilization?"

"A few."

That made her eyes open. "Are you serious or just trying to make me feel better?"

"I'm serious. There have been hikers through here in the past few weeks, probably following the stream as we have been. This could even be an established hiking trail, though I doubt there are many hikers out with this weather threatening. We're probably no more than ten miles from a road of some sort."

"Ten miles?"

"Just a guess, of course."

"Your guesses have been on target so far. We should be able to walk ten miles today, shouldn't we?"

Again, that telltale hesitation before he answered. "Under normal circumstances, sure. With the shape we're both in, maybe. If the rain starts again as heavily as I think it's going to, we'll have to find shelter again. Spring storms can be dangerous, especially around this stream.''

''Do you think there's *any* chance there are rescuers looking for us in this area?'' she asked with a wistful note she couldn't quite conceal.

''There's always a chance.''

She couldn't take much encouragement from his tone. She closed her eyes and tried to gather strength to start walking again. Her head pounded and every inch of her body ached. It was so tempting to just let herself slide into sleep and stay there. Oblivion was sounding better all the time.

She felt Donovan stroke her hair again. She felt the tension in his leg, and knew she was causing him concern again. She was sorry about that, but she just couldn't put on a strong front at the moment. She hoped to be able to do so again after a brief rest.

She had just convinced herself to open her eyes again when the first raindrop hit her cheek. It was followed by more, becoming a light rain punctuated with increasingly loud claps of thunder.

''We have to find shelter,'' Donovan urged. ''We can't risk being out in the open or beneath a tree in case of lightning. There's a rock overhang a few yards away. We'll huddle under that until the storm passes, okay?''

Had it just been herself, she might well have lain right there and dared the lightning to hit her. The thought of forcing herself to her feet was almost enough to make her wish it would. But Donovan's safety was at risk, too, she reminded herself.

She pushed herself upright. "I'll help you up," she said, forcibly ignoring the dizziness.

His attempt to smile came across more like a grimace. "We'll help each other."

Doing so had gotten them this far, she reminded herself. No matter how tempting the thought might be, she couldn't give up as long as Donovan still depended on her.

Chapter Eleven

Wallace Childers's florid face was covered in a film of sweat, his muddy brown eyes were bulging with panic. An outside observer might think he was in fear for his life, though the two well-dressed men who faced him had been almost excessively polite when they had invited him to sit and "chat" with them.

Several suitcases were stacked behind him, testifying to his activity just before his uninvited guests had arrived so dramatically. Twenty minutes later and they would have missed him altogether.

"You've got this all wrong, Falcon," he blustered, speaking to the man he considered to be the most dangerous. "I had nothing to do with the disappearance of your—"

"Childers," Bryan cut in, his voice very soft but quite clear. "I think you should reconsider the rest of that sentence. You see, Jason and I aren't debating about whether to have you arrested for arranging a kidnapping.''

Standing behind his seated employer, his arms crossed over his chest, his face totally impassive, Jason Colby shook his head.

"You aren't?''

"No. We've actually been discussing whether we should let you live.''

Childers jerked as if he'd been shocked by an electric current. "You can't just burst into my apartment and threaten my life!'' he shouted, waving a trembling hand at the door that still hung precariously from its broken hinges.

"You're absolutely right,'' Bryan agreed pleasantly. "Why don't you call the police?''

There was a lengthy silence in the room. No one moved.

Childers's eyes jumped from the telephone to the two deceptively relaxed-looking men waiting for him to make a move. Standing just inside the open doorway, almost quivering with the suppressed urge to speak, stood a young woman with brown hair and furious hazel eyes. A woman who looked so much like Chloe Pennington that Childers had nearly fainted when he'd first seen her.

He swallowed hard. "I told you, already. I don't know where your friends are.''

"Perhaps you should think a bit harder,'' Bryan prodded.

From the doorway, the woman spoke impatiently. "He's not going to help us. Just kill him, Colby.''

Childers could almost feel the blood drain from his face as Jason Colby looked fully prepared to follow the woman's suggestion.

Though Bryan's mouth twitched with what might have been a hint of a smile, he held up a hand without looking around at his companions. "Grace—you promised not to speak," he reminded her, causing her to subside into resentful silence again. "And Jason follows my instructions alone. Now, Mr. Childers— perhaps you'd like to start over? *Where are my friends?*"

The narrow rock ledge above them provided little protection from the driving rain, but maybe it gave them some shelter from the lightning that ripped across the charcoal-colored sky above them. At least, Donovan hoped he hadn't made another mistake by stuffing them into this hollow.

Holding Chloe in his arms, he had his back turned as much as possible to the outside, trying to shield her from the rain that blew in on them. His back was soaked, his hair dripping. Chloe wasn't much drier, but at least he seemed to be taking the brunt of it.

As often as he had urged her not to give up during the past three days, he found himself teetering on the verge of doing so now. Maybe he'd been in worse situations—he couldn't remember at the moment— but it was Chloe's suffering that was ripping his heart out.

She'd tried so hard, but she had just about reached her limits. And he hadn't been a hell of a lot of help to her—first letting her get kidnapped, then leading her into the forest, idiotically hurting his leg, bringing her into the sights of a crazy man's shotgun, and now sitting with her in the middle of a damned lightning storm.

Bryan wouldn't have to fire him when this was

over, he decided. He was going to quit. He didn't deserve to keep a position of responsibility and trust.

Maybe he could build himself a lean-to in another deserted forest somewhere.

The air crackled around him as a bolt of lightning sliced through the forest nearby. The crash of thunder competed with the sound of splitting wood and hammering rain. Donovan could smell the ozone in the air and feel the hairs standing up on his arms and the back of his neck. He could only hope again that the ledge would protect them.

The way his luck had been running, it would more likely fall on them, he thought glumly.

Cradled against his shoulder, Chloe moaned a little, then stirred, interrupting his private orgy of self-recrimination.

"I must have fallen asleep," she said, her voice thick.

"Only for a few minutes. Go ahead and rest. There's nothing else to do until this storm breaks."

"I've been thinking about that," she said. "At least, I *was* thinking about it before I fell asleep."

"Thinking about what?"

"When the storm is over. Even with your injured leg, you've been making better time than I have today, since this stupid fever keeps making me so dizzy. If you leave me here, maybe you can—"

"I'm not leaving you."

Though his sharp tone had been intended to stop any argument, she persisted anyway. "Think about it before you say no, Donovan. You said yourself we're probably close to a road."

"I could be wrong. It was a total guess."

"I know, but you could be right. If we wait much

longer, we're both going to be too weak and too sick to walk at all. God knows how, considering your leg and all, but you're still holding up pretty well. You're the logical one to go for help."

"Chloe, I am not leaving you in the forest alone with a high fever. End of discussion."

She sighed. "All right. I'll try to keep walking as soon as the storm is over."

"I know it won't be easy, but you have to try. We have to get you to help as quickly as possible. Infections can be…well, they can be dangerous."

She bit her lip, probably remembering what he'd told her about his mother. "It's probably just a passing fever. Or weakness from not eating. I'm sure I'll be able to go on after resting for a while. I just thought it would be quicker if you—"

"If I have to carry you on my back, I'm not leaving you here alone."

She didn't speak again for a while. They listened to the storm, shivered when cold rain blew in on them, and dealt silently with their individual mental and physical discomforts. Donovan was just about to start another silent litany of his failings when Chloe broke the silence between them again with a request that caught him completely by surprise. "Tell me why you hate to be called a bodyguard."

"What?"

"I need to talk to take my mind off my problems."

"So you want to talk about my problems instead?"

"Is being called a bodyguard a problem for you?"

"It's just inaccurate. Bryan didn't ask me to serve as your bodyguard when I picked you up the other day. I was simply supposed to drive you to his house and wait with you there until he arrived."

"I know. You've explained all that. But you still haven't explained why you get all tense when I use the word. Have you worked as a bodyguard before?"

"Briefly." He looked out at the rain and hoped his short reply would discourage her from asking more.

It didn't, of course.

"What went wrong?"

"The person I was guarding got killed. I ignored my instincts, and went along with him when he insisted that I leave him alone with his girlfriend for a few hours. He was tired of being guarded all the time, thought he would be safe for a while in the hideaway we had selected for him, and he convinced me that he would be safe there—but he wasn't."

"You were working for the man who was killed?" she asked, trying to follow the terse story.

"Yes."

"And he asked you to leave him alone for a few hours?"

"I shouldn't have listened. I should have insisted I stay with him."

"Donovan, you can't blame yourself for following your employer's orders. It sounds as though he made the mistake, not you."

Staring blindly into the rain, he shook his head. "I was hired to protect him. I failed. He died. I'm not the only one who blamed me for that failure."

"The only person who should be blamed is the killer. Was he ever caught?"

"Yeah. Lot of good that did my client."

"Who was your client? A friend?"

"No. A man who'd made some powerful enemies on his way to fame. You would probably know the name if I mentioned it, but it doesn't matter now. That ended my bodyguard career.''

"Was that when you went to work for Bryan?"

He shrugged. "I bummed around for a few years after that, taking some assignments I'd just as soon not discuss now for some people who operated just barely within the range of the law. My reputation was going downhill fast when Bryan tracked me down and convinced me to join him."

He hadn't planned to tell her all that. But maybe now she could understand the intensity of his loyalty to Bryan. Why he wouldn't do anything to jeopardize that relationship.

Maybe she could also understand that he wasn't exactly what anyone would consider a hero—just in case she had made the mistake of thinking of him in that light during the past few days.

"No more talk," he said abruptly, twisting to arrange his injured leg in a slightly more comfortable position—which meant sticking it straight out into the rain. "Get some rest. You're going to need it."

Donovan waited until he was sure the rain had stopped for a while before he suggested they move on. It took all the strength Chloe had to make herself climb to her feet and start walking beside him. He hovered nearby to give her support, though he leaned so heavily on his walking stick that he looked as though he needed a great deal of support himself.

They made a pathetic sight, she couldn't help thinking as they pushed on one halting step at a time. She didn't want to think about what she must look like with her stringy hair, assorted bruises and clothes that would go straight into a trash can if she made it out of here. Donovan was unshaven, his hair limp and damp from the rain, his black clothing dirty and torn, his leg bound in boards and scraps of coral-colored cloth. Beneath his whiskers, she could see a dark bruise on his left cheek from his fight with the kidnapper.

Yet as battered as he looked at the moment, she had a feeling there wasn't a woman alive who would dismiss him without a second glance. He was bruised and weary, but competence and power still seemed to surround him like an invisible mantle. A battle-scarred warrior, she mused. Battered, but unbroken.

And then she made a face and shook her head in response to her fanciful mental ramblings. Maybe her fever was climbing again.

"Is something funny?" Donovan asked, proving how closely he'd been watching her.

"Look at us," she retorted. "Don't you find us a funny sight?"

He glanced down at himself, then at her. His mouth twitched in that little smile she found herself watching for so often. "Not many women would find anything about this picture amusing."

"I've decided to attribute my amusement to fever. I seem to be suffering delusions."

"Don't suppose you could hallucinate us a cup of coffee?"

"I'll try. Having a caffeine attack?"

He reached out to push the low-hanging limbs of a tree out of their way. "There are a lot of things I'd like to have right now, but a cup of coffee definitely tops the—"

His words ended abruptly. From behind him, Chloe studied his suddenly still back. "What is it?"

"A road."

"A road?" She hurried to catch up with him, hardly even wincing when she stepped on a rock. "Where?"

He nodded ahead. "An old logging road, from the look of it. But it's been used recently. Four-wheelers, at a guess. ATVs."

She stared in some dismay at the rutted dirt track Donovan had generously called a road. "How do we know which way to follow it?"

Limping forward, he studied the tracks, then pointed. "That way. South."

Frowning, she looked in that direction. Trees, hills, and more trees lay ahead—both directions. "Why south?"

"It leads out."

She looked again at the track. "And you know this how?"

He shrugged.

She studied his impassive face for a moment before asking, "Do you really have a reason to choose that direction, or are you just making a guess?"

"Look at it this way. I have a fifty-fifty chance of being right."

After a moment, she nodded. "Okay. We'll go south."

Making a gallant motion with his left hand, he said, "After you."

She drew a deep breath as she stepped onto one hard-packed track and turned to follow it. It was a road, she reminded herself. It had to lead somewhere.

It was no easier making their way along the old road than it had been across the forest floor. Thick mud made walking slippery and brush and vines tangled around their ankles.

Chloe was hit with several more dizzy spells, forcing her to stop and rest several times. Donovan stumbled twice, almost falling, and scaring her half to death. She was so afraid he was going to further hurt his leg, shatter the cracked bone so that it pierced the skin or caused him some permanent disability. Both times he managed to catch himself with his crutch.

Her steps slowed to a near-crawl, and she suspected she couldn't walk a straight line in a sobriety test. The world was doing funny things around her, the lines waving, merging, creating a surreal landscape straight out of a Dali painting. She wasn't hallucinating—exactly—but she wasn't exactly coherent, either. She hoped it was a good sign that she was aware of her condition.

"We're going to have to stop," Donovan said, sliding his left arm around her. "You can't go any farther."

"I can keep going," she said, staring fiercely at the road ahead.

"Not without collapsing. Come on, we can sit beneath that big tree if it isn't too muddy."

She shook her head, irrationally afraid that if she sat down she wouldn't get up again. "We have to keep walking or we won't get out."

"We'll get out, Chloe." His voice was unusually gentle. "You just need to rest a little while. And so do I, okay?"

"What time is it?" she asked as he led her toward the tree he'd indicated.

"I don't know. It's so cloudy it's hard to tell. It was about seven when we started walking, and the rainstorm lasted maybe an hour—it's probably around noon.''

"It feels later. Do you think it's going to rain again?''

He glanced at the sky before turning to help her sit down on the damp moss beneath the tree. "Probably. There were predictions for a lot of rain this week.''

"I know. Grace pointed it out to me several times, asking me how much fun I thought it would be to spend a week of vacation watching rain fall.''

"I'm sure you'd have found something more interesting to do than that.''

He'd kept his voice uninflected, but she bristled a little, anyway. Or she would have, if she hadn't been so tired and so sick. "Bryan and I were going to talk,'' she murmured, leaning her head back against the tree. "Just get to know each other better. That's all there was to it.''

"You'd have had a nice time. Bryan can be very good company.''

Donovan's bland tone was starting to annoy her. She decided to let the conversation end before exhaustion and fever made her say something she might regret later.

He didn't seem to be listening to her anyway.

After their awkward conversation, Donovan seemed impatient to start hiking again. He allowed only a short rest before he asked Chloe if she felt like moving on again. She didn't, of course, but she struggled to her feet. Donovan believed they were close to rescue, and she had learned to trust his instincts.

The walk seemed to get harder as they pressed on. The ground grew progressively muddier and slipperier as the grass on the packed-dirt trail became sparser. Chloe hoped that meant the road had been used more in that area recently, which could mean they were getting closer to a populated area.

And then the rain began again, this time a slow, misty drizzle that was just heavy enough to make them soggy, chilled and uncomfortable.

Chloe had walked almost as far as she physically could when she heard Donovan growl something incomprehensible—something she was probably better off not asking him to clarify, judging by his tone. Looking forward, she saw what had upset him.

The torrential rains of the past two days had flooded a fast-running section of the stream, causing the roiling, tumbling water to completely cover the road ahead of them. The road had fallen off into a deep ditch dug by previous floods. In late summer, the stream was probably quite shallow here, just enough to give the ATV riders a good splash. Now it might as well have been a river blocking them from the other side of the road.

For several long, silent moments, Donovan stood unmoving, staring at the rushing water as if he could hardly believe he was really seeing it. And then he erupted in fury, slamming his walking stick to the ground and letting loose a string of colorful curses that made Chloe's eyebrows rise.

So Donovan could lose his composure occasionally. She'd wondered about that. This latest setback was apparently the last straw for him.

She stepped in to soothe him before he hurt himself. "We'll find a way around it," she said, laying a hand on his arm.

"There is no way around it. Look at the bluffs we'd have to climb if we go upstream. Or the steep slopes we'd have to descend downstream. Why do you think this road runs where it does? It's the only relatively level path.''

He'd spoken through clenched teeth, obviously trying to get himself back under control. "Then we'll wade through it,'' she suggested. ''We'll help each other across. It couldn't be that deep.''

"It isn't how deep it is, it's how fast it's moving. One misstep and we'd be swept downstream.''

"We could wait here, find a place to take shelter until the stream goes down some.''

He looked up at the sky. The drizzle was becoming heavier now, and showed no signs of ending soon. "That could be a while. Days, maybe.''

"We don't seem to have a whole lot of choices.''

"That thought has occurred to me.''

She stepped to the edge of the erosion-carved ravine and looked down, watching the increasingly heavy rain merging into the surging flood waters. The temperature was falling again; or maybe it just felt that way because she was so wet and tired. She shivered and wrapped her arms around herself in a futile attempt at warmth.

Donovan stepped beside her, placing a hand on her shoulder. "I'm sorry,'' he said, his voice calmer now. "I shouldn't have snapped at you just because I'm frustrated.''

She offered him a tentative smile. "You deserve to blow off steam sometimes.''

"Still, I shouldn't have—''

Their combined weight must have been too much for the waterlogged ground at the edge of the gully. Before Donovan could finish his sentence, the earth gave way beneath their feet.

Chapter Twelve

Maybe they could have caught themselves if they hadn't already been in such weakened condition. Or maybe not. The ground literally fell from under them, tumbling into the hungry stream which took them with it.

Chloe went into the water on her back. She was immediately swept downstream, crashing against rocks and the dirt sides, struggling to get her face above the surface. Her first gasp for breath ended with a mouthful of water. Choking and gagging, she went under again.

The water was no more than four feet deep but running so fast she couldn't keep her feet beneath her when she tried to stand. She slammed hard into another large rock, tried to grab it, but had her grip torn away by the force of the water. The current was too strong, the ground too uneven and slippery to give her a grip. All she could do was go with the flow and try to gulp air whenever her face broke the water.

Something snagged her shirt, jerking her to a stop. She scrabbled to catch hold of it, her hands closing around something hard and slick. Tree roots, she realized as she gulped air, trying to focus through water, rain and tears. The flood had washed the dirt away from the bottom of a large tree, leaving long, bare roots extending out into the water.

It took all her strength to cling to the roots and keep herself from being swept away again. She didn't know how far she had been carried by the floodwaters, or how long she'd been battling them. The heavy gray sky pressed down above her and rain fell in windswept sheets around her. All she could see was the forest and the bluffs rising around her.

She couldn't see Donovan.

Whipping her head from one side to the other, she searched desperately for any sign of him. "Donovan?"

She could barely hear her own voice over the sounds of the rain and rushing water. She called louder, "Donovan!"

She couldn't help thinking of his injured leg. What if he'd been pushed under the water when they were first swept in? Even now he could be trapped, struggling to get his head above water, slowly losing consciousness...

"Donovan!"

She tried dragging herself out of the water, but her hands kept sliding on the slick roots. She lodged herself firmly into a notch among them and rested a moment, panting.

Her head was spinning now, and she felt as though

she could very easily faint again, but she fought off the dizziness. She had to find Donovan.

She tried calling him again. "Donovan!"

"Chloe?"

She jerked her head around so quickly that dizziness almost overwhelmed her again, loosening her grip on the roots. She scrambled to regain her hold, clinging so tightly her hands ached.

"Donovan?" Had she only imagined she'd heard him? Was it only desperate, wishful thinking?

"Chloe—where are you?"

It was definitely his voice, she thought with a choked cry of relief. He was all right. Somehow he'd gotten out of the water.

She tried again to pull herself out, but she was unsuccessful. She called out to him again and waited, hanging on while Donovan made his way to her. She could hear him now, crashing through the brush, his occasional muted curses drifting to her on wet gusts of wind.

It took him a while to reach her. When she finally saw him, she understood why.

The left side of his face was covered with rain-streaked blood from a cut at his temple. His right leg dragged so badly that he was almost hopping on his left. He looked as though he was in terrible pain, but he also looked as close to frantic as she had seen him to this point.

He didn't see her at first. "Chloe?"

"I'm here."

He limped toward her. She called out again.

Finally spotting her, he stopped, his shoulders seeming to sag in relief for a moment. "Are you all right?"

"I think so. But I can't get out."

"Hang on." He made his way carefully toward her. Stopping on the bank, he rested a hand on the trunk of the tree and looked down at her. "I'm going to try to pull you out. You'll have to hold very tightly to make sure you aren't swept away again."

"How did you get out?"

"I hit a shallow area, grabbed a tree branch." His foot slipped on a patch of mud, but he caught himself quickly. He steadied himself with one hand wrapped around a sturdy limb and leaned toward her, his other hand outstretched. "Brace your foot against the root and push toward me. Catch my hand and don't let go."

The position he was in had his weight almost fully on his right leg, which had to be causing him agony. Yet she knew he wouldn't falter as he helped her out, no matter how bad the pain. Once again, she trusted him with her life.

He hadn't let her down so far.

Somehow, she managed to place her hand in his. Somehow, he found the strength to drag her out of the water.

They stumbled away from the crumbling edge. And then they fell limply to a wet, grassy patch of ground, both too tired to stand, clinging to each other as though they were afraid to let go again. Lying there in the rain, Donovan buried his face in her dripping hair, while she burrowed into the wet curve of his throat. She felt heavy tremors running through him. She didn't know whether to attribute them to cold, pain, exhaustion, reaction or—as in her case—a combination of all those things.

He drew back far enough to cup her face in his

hands, studying her with anxious eyes. "You're sure you're all right?"

"I'm fine." She reached up to touch her fingertips to the deep cut on his forehead. "How did this happen?"

His shrug was impatient, dismissing his latest injury as unimportant. "I saw you go under. I never saw you come back up."

"It took me a while. The force of the water kept shoving me back down."

"You could have drowned." His voice was suddenly bleak. "I was afraid you had."

"I thought the same about you," she whispered. "I was so afraid for you."

"We're okay now. It's over."

"Yes." She tried to give him a smile. She couldn't quite manage it.

A new look of panic flitted across his face as he leaned over her. "Don't cry, Chloe. We're safe."

"I'm not crying," she insisted. She was sure the moisture on her cheeks were raindrops, not tears. Until her breath caught in a sob. And then another.

Donovan groaned. "Damn it, Chloe."

He touched his lips to one of her rain-and-tear-streaked cheeks, and then the other. His mouth felt so warm against her icy skin—and yet she shivered in reaction to his touch.

When his lips settled on hers, she forgot all about the rain and the cold, her aches and pains, and their bleak situation. She simply wrapped her arms around his neck and allowed herself to get lost again. This time she didn't even try to find her way to safety.

Their lips had touched before, but this was the first

time he had really kissed her. And it answered one question once and for all—

Donovan really did kiss as skillfully as he did everything else.

His lips were hard. Hungry. Either his emotions were being influenced by the dramatic near-miss they had just survived or this kiss had been building for a long time. She knew which one was the case for her.

Four days ago, this man had been a complete stranger to her. Sometime between that day and now, she had managed to fall in love with him.

She had waited so long for it to happen to her. She had almost given up hoping that it ever would. How could she have known that love would find her so soon after she'd finally stopped searching for it?

He lifted his head only a fraction of an inch and started to speak. Chloe wasn't quite ready to hear what he might have said. She drew him back down to her.

He kissed her again, but something had changed this time. She sensed him trying to gather himself, trying to get his needs under control. Donovan wasn't a man to let himself get swept away for very long, if ever.

She didn't try to stop him when he pulled away this time. He rolled to his back, letting the rain pelt his face for a moment before he shoved himself upright.

"We should walk as far as we can before dark," he said, his voice impassive, his face expressionless. "We're both too wet to worry about the rain now, anyway, so finding shelter wouldn't do us much good. And you're shivering. You'll probably warm up quicker if we're moving than if we sit still."

She knew he must be fully aware that her trembling had little to do with being cold, but he seemed to be pretending nothing earth-shattering had just happened between them. "Donovan?"

"At least we're on the other side of the stream," he said, half turning to look back at the water. "Not exactly the way I would have preferred to cross, of course."

"Donovan, I—"

Still without meeting her eyes, he offered her a hand. "Here. Let me help you up."

He wasn't going to talk about it. Not now, anyway. She took his hand, but was careful to support her own weight as she rose slowly. "Do you know how to get back to the road?"

"Yes. You really weren't carried very far by the water. Not as far as it probably seemed to you."

"The rain seems to be letting up a little."

He moved a spreading bush aside and held it until she moved past. "Yeah. I think it's about to stop. It's about time we had a little luck. Watch your feet. It looks slippery ahead."

It was ridiculous that they were discussing the weather, she thought as she glared fiercely at the ground ahead. How could he kiss her the way he had and then start talking about the chances of rain?

He was right, of course, to change the subject. This was hardly the time to discuss the future—at least any future beyond getting out of these woods.

And still she heard herself saying, "I'm not going to marry Bryan."

Donovan hesitated a few moments, then stumbled on. "That's between you and Bryan. But I still don't think you should make a decision of that magnitude under these conditions.''

''I'm not being impulsive. My decision would have been no different even if we hadn't been kidnapped.''

He stepped carefully over a fallen tree trunk, grimacing when he was forced to put his weight down on his right leg. ''Let's just concentrate on getting out of here, shall we?''

He moved ahead of her, and she looked at his back. His shoulders were squared, his spine very straight, even though his steps were slow and halting. He had withdrawn from her mentally, emotionally *and* physically.

Her instincts warned her not to push him. He was the one who obviously needed time to process what had happened between them. Maybe it wasn't as easy for him to identify his emotions as it had been for her when she'd been struck with that stunning revelation that she was in love with him.

Remembering the unguarded look on his face when he had first seen her after fearing that she'd drowned, she told herself that he had to feel something. Replaying those passionate kisses in her mind, she wanted to believe that his feelings were as strong as her own. It was the possibility that she was wrong—that she had only read into the kisses what she wanted to find there—that kept her quiet now.

As badly as she wanted to be rescued, she couldn't help wondering if leaving this forest would also mean saying goodbye to Donovan.

After finding the dirt road again, they struggled along without giving each other much assistance, since neither of them was in much better shape than the other. It had stopped raining again, though the air was still so heavy and damp that it was almost like breathing water.

Wet and cold, miserable and edgy, Chloe winced in pain with every step. She knew Donovan was hurting every bit as badly—if not more so—though he didn't complain. He didn't say *anything,* actually. He just limped on, his face grim, his movements determined.

He'd become the uncommunicative stranger again. Only this time she sensed that he was having to make an effort to remain that way. Now that he had reached out to her, she thought he would have liked to do so again. She could only speculate about his reasons for withdrawing so abruptly—loyalty to Bryan, uncertainty of her feelings, fear of the future or baggage from his past. All of the above.

"It's getting so dark," she gasped after stumbling into a rut and nearly falling on her face. "I can't see where we're going. Shouldn't we find another cave or someplace to spend the night?"

"Try to make it just a little farther."

Was he uncomfortable with the idea of spending another night in a cave with her? They'd spent three nights in each other's arms now, their feelings escalating each night—was he afraid of what might happen if they spent another night that way?

Personally, she didn't think he had much to worry about. She was so tired she suspected she might become comatose the moment she stopped moving.

She started to tell him so, but he reached out suddenly to grab her arm. "What—?"

"Look—over that way."

Frowning in bewilderment, she followed the direction of his pointing finger. ''I don't—oh, my God. Is that—?''

''Yes. Come on.''

He hadn't let go of her arm. Half supporting her, half dragging her, he led them off the road and across a rocky clearing toward the small, battered-looking mobile home they had spotted.

Her heart pounded against her chest, and her breath caught in excited half gasps, half sobs. *Rescue,* she thought. Only now did she admit that she had begun to wonder if it would ever happen.

It took them a good fifteen minutes to make their way across the rough clearing to the trailer. There were no lights on in the windows, and Chloe had the distinct feeling that no one was inside. The feeling was confirmed when Donovan pounded on the front door and no one answered.

''Now what?'' she asked wearily.

''We break in,'' he answered, as if it should have been obvious to her.

''Just—break in?''

''Under the circumstances, I don't think anyone would blame us. And if I cause any damage, I'll pay for it. I just hope there's a phone in there. At the very least, we can get dry and warm.''

Because dry and warm sounded so appealing at the moment—not to mention the prospect of a telephone—she stood aside without further comment and watched him efficiently break into the locked trailer.

She no longer even questioned where he'd learned the skills he'd displayed during the past few days. She was just glad he'd picked them up somewhere in his undoubtedly colorful adventures.

Motioning for her to wait a minute, Donovan stepped inside first. "Hello?" he called out.

Silence was his only answer. He groped at the wall near the door, and a moment later light flooded the main room of the trailer. "We have electricity," he announced with satisfaction.

Her knees almost went weak in relief. She moved in behind him. The room was furnished in a style she could only think of as "early garage sale"—but it *was* warm and dry.

"I would speculate that this is someone's hunting and fishing retreat," Donovan said, glancing around the sparsely decorated trailer. "We must be close to a river—probably the one that stream empties into. And I'd guess we aren't very far from other people."

"Thank God. Is there a phone?"

"Not that I've seen yet. I'll check the back rooms, you look in the kitchen."

"I'm dripping all over the carpet."

Donovan glanced down at the ragged green shag carpeting beneath their feet. "I'm sure it's not the first time it's been dripped on. Don't worry about it."

"I know. You'll buy him new carpet, right?"

"Hell, I'll buy him a new trailer," he answered rashly. "Check the kitchen."

It felt so good to flip a switch and have lights come on as a result. She didn't see a telephone, but there was a sink, an old electric range and a small refrigerator/freezer combination. The fridge hummed; she opened the door and cool air brushed her wet skin, making her shiver and smile at the same time.

Closing the refrigerator door, she moved to the sink and twisted the left knob. After a moment, warm water cascaded over her hand. She could have a hot bath, she realized in delight. The prospect made her almost giddy.

A thick quilt was draped suddenly over her shoulders. Clutching it around her, she turned to find Donovan standing behind her. "Did you find a phone?"

"No. But there are some men's clothes in one of the bedrooms. Jeans, flannel shirts, a couple pair of shoes. No shower, but a bathtub with hot water. And I found a real treasure under the sink—bars of soap, packages of disposable razors, several new toothbrushes still in the packaging. Why don't you take a hot bath and put on some dry clothes while I look around for clues about where we are."

Toothbrushes. If her feet hadn't hurt so badly, she might have bounced in anticipation. She settled for a smile. "I feel a little odd about raiding someone's closet without permission—but I'm sure you'll buy him a whole new wardrobe when we get back to civilization."

He almost smiled. "Absolutely."

"Then I'll ignore my scruples and take you up on that suggestion." She smiled in anticipation as she hobbled past him.

"Chloe." Donovan caught her arm when she would have passed him.

She looked up at him. He pressed a hand to her forehead, testing for fever. Their faces were very close together and for a moment she saw real emotion in his bright-green eyes. A quiver of response ran through her. But then he masked whatever he was feeling, released her, and stepped back. "You're still running a fever. I didn't see any aspirin in the bathroom, but I'll look around in the rest of the trailer, see what I can find while you're taking your bath."

She nodded and left the room as quickly as her battered feet would allow.

Donovan was waiting outside the bathroom door when Chloe finally emerged. He'd begun to worry that she'd been in there too long. For all he knew, she could have passed out in the tub or something. He was too tired and stressed to consider how unlikely it was that, having survived a flooded stream, she would drown in a bathtub.

Her hair was wet again, but looked squeaky clean this time. Her fresh-scrubbed skin was starkly pale, except for the purple smudges beneath her eyes. She wore a big flannel shirt that almost swallowed her, falling all the way to her knees. Her poor battered feet were bare, revealing all the abuse they had taken in those woods.

The big shirt made her look small in comparison. Delicate. Almost fragile. He knew first-hand how deceptive that impression could be.

He remembered the first day he'd met her, when he'd thought of her as more pretty than beautiful. Funny how that impression had changed during the past few days. Now he was convinced that he'd never seen a more attractive woman.

"I found coffee in the kitchen, and I brewed a pot," he said, his voice a bit brusque. "And I heated some canned soup. I also found a first-aid kit stuffed in one of the kitchen cabinets. I set out a bottle of acetaminophen. Take a couple to reduce your fever and then you can eat while I bathe. After that, we'll see about treating some of your wounds."

She nodded in response to his list of directions. "Soup and coffee sound good," she admitted. "The hot bath warmed my outside, but I still feel cold inside.''

He smiled a little, as she had hoped he would, but it was hard for him to find any humor in what she had been through. ''The food is in the kitchen. Have all you want, I've already eaten. I'll hurry with my bath and join you in a few minutes.''

''Don't hurry. Trust me, it feels too good to be clean again to rush through it.''

''I'll keep that in mind.''

He watched her walk away, taking a moment to appreciate the graceful sway of her hips. Even walking on shredded feet, she carried herself like a princess, he thought—then scowled at his uncharacteristic fancifulness as he turned to lock himself in the bathroom.

A short while later, bathed, clean-shaven, dressed in a flannel shirt that was too short in the sleeves and jeans that were too big in the waist, Donovan ran his tongue over his brushed teeth and reminded himself to reward the owner of this trailer generously.

He'd removed the waterlogged, rigged-up splint before his bath. His leg was about three different shades of purple, but the painkillers he'd taken while he was making the coffee had eased the throbbing somewhat. He didn't know if his leg was broken, cracked or bruised to the bone, but he figured it wouldn't fall off before he could have it treated.

The cut at his temple had stopped bleeding, but that was a new lump and bruise to add to his collection. In his ongoing battle with nature, the other side was definitely a few licks ahead, he thought in resignation.

He found Chloe in the living room, sitting on the couch cross-legged with the first-aid kit beside her.

She was making some rather odd contortions in an attempt to see the bottom of her feet.

"I told you I would help you with that," he said, moving toward her as quickly as his own injuries would allow.

She must not have heard him approaching. Hurriedly making sure the big flannel shirt covered her adequately, she tucked an almost-dry strand of hair behind her ear and asked, "Why did you take off your splint?"

"I couldn't take a bath in it."

"I'll help you get it back on."

"Never mind. I'm not sure it was helping much, anyway."

"But—"

"Forget it, Chloe. Let's see about your feet." He sat beside her and reached for the first-aid kit. "Did you have enough to eat?"

"Yes, plenty, thank you. The soup was wonderful."

"Straight out of a can. You were just hungry enough for anything to taste good."

"You're probably right."

"Give me your feet."

"That sounds a bit odd," she murmured, even as she turned sideways on the couch and complied.

Donovan ordered himself to keep a tight lid on his emotions as he reached for her right foot and rested it on his knee. Even making a fierce effort to be completely objective and impersonal, he couldn't help noticing that her feet were small, high-arched and perfectly formed.

And so bruised and torn that the sight of them made his chest ache. "Damn, these must have hurt," he muttered, running a fingertip very lightly over her scarred and peeling sole.

She squirmed and laughed softly. "That tickled."

"Sorry," he said, but he had liked hearing her laugh. He would bet she did so often under the right circumstances—and in more entertaining company.

Frowning, he set to work with antibiotic ointment and bandages, covering the worst of the cuts. Two cuts looked badly infected; he suspected they would have to be treated by medical professionals. "I hope you're current on your tetanus shots."

"I am."

"Good." He reached for her left foot. To his relief, it didn't seem to be as badly damaged, though there were several deep scratches around her ankle. Looked as though she'd tangled with a thorny vine. He spread ointment on those wounds, as well, still trying to keep his mind off the intimacy of their position.

Not to mention the fact that she was wearing nothing but a large flannel shirt.

Either his awkwardness was affecting her or she, too, was trying to divert herself when she asked, "Why do you suppose the electricity is turned on in this trailer? D'you think the owner leaves it on all the time, even when he isn't here?"

"He's probably been here recently—maybe even last weekend. Probably fishes nearby."

"If he comes often, then he probably doesn't live very far away. We must be getting closer to civilization."

"I think you're right." Satisfied that he'd treated every visible cut, he looked up from her feet. "Any other injuries you need me to treat?"

Her smile was suddenly wicked. Before he could

predict what she was going to do, she leaned forward and wrapped her arms around his neck. ''Just one,'' she murmured against his lips. And then kissed him.

Oh, hell. He was only human. Dragging her against him, he slanted his mouth to a better angle and took her up on what she was offering.

Chapter Thirteen

Chloe's lips had been ice-cold when Donovan had pulled her from that stream. Now they were warm enough to sear a brand on his soul…if he wasn't careful. But maybe it was too late for caution.

She murmured her pleasure with his response and snuggled closer, so that it was too damned obvious she wasn't wearing a bra beneath the shirt. Or anything else, most likely. His hands wandered almost without volition, stroking her smooth thighs, her softly curved hips and slender waist. Her breasts were on the small side, but firm and high—just the right size to fill his hands when he smoothed them slowly upward.

Pressing herself into his touch, Chloe locked her hands in his damp hair, and kissed him as though she had been starved more for him than for food.

Being wanted so badly was intoxicating. Made him

feel special. Almost like a man who deserved a woman like Chloe.

He started to pull back. She tightened her grip and parted her lips for him. There was no way he could resist the temptation to deepen the kiss. Just for a moment, he promised himself.

One taste and he was lost.

The too-loose borrowed jeans grew significantly tighter as his tongue plunged repeatedly into her mouth to mate with hers. Her hands were suddenly all over him, stroking, exploring, testing his strength. She seemed to take as much pleasure from touching him as he did her—and that, too, was a heady sensation.

He tried to remind himself that she was endowing him with qualities he didn't possess. That she was turning him into some sort of hero because they had grown so dependent on each other during their ordeal. Yet when she kissed him like this, he found it all too easy to believe she wanted him for exactly who he was. Flaws, baggage and all.

That sort of self-deception was dangerous. Addictive. He'd never even been tempted to indulge in it before.

Everything was different with Chloe. She tempted him in ways he'd never been tempted before.

She almost tempted him to forget she was the woman his best friend planned to marry.

The thought of Bryan gave him the willpower to rip his mouth from Chloe's. "We can't do this."

She blinked and moistened her lips with the tip of her tongue—a gesture that almost shattered his sanity again. "Are you in pain?" she asked, her voice bedroom-husky.

"Oh, yeah," he groaned, pushing himself away from her. How had they ended up sprawled in this position, with her on her back and him draped over her? He didn't even remember moving.

Rising to her elbows, she studied him anxiously. "Is it your leg? Have you twisted it?"

"My leg is fine." It hurt like hell, of course, now that his attention had been called to it, but he welcomed the pain. It gave him something to concentrate on besides the throbbing ache in his groin.

She reached out to brush her fingertips through the lock of hair that habitually tumbled onto his forehead, being careful to avoid the swollen bump at his temple. "You're being macho again, aren't you? I know your leg is hurting."

He pulled away from her gentle touch, sliding to the other end of the couch. He wasn't quite ready to stand. "I'll take some more painkillers. Why don't you go lie down for a while? I want to look around for a way to get us out of here."

"And after we get out?" she asked, keeping her gaze locked on his face.

After that, he thought, they would go their separate ways. She would get over this danger-induced crush she seemed to have developed for him, and she would probably marry Bryan. And he would have to figure out how to spend the rest of his life avoiding his best friend's wife. The woman who was everything he could have wanted—had things been different. Had *he* been different.

"Get some rest, Chloe," he said again, refusing to meet her eyes. "By tomorrow you'll be home."

"Home," she murmured. "Where is home for you, Donovan? I don't even know."

"I don't have a home." He had an apartment, of course, but he thought of it as a place to sleep, a place to store his stuff. Not home. "I haven't wanted one."

"Everyone wants a home."

"Not everyone." He finally stood, balancing his weight carefully on his left leg. "Go to bed. We're both tired and keyed up. Things will look different tomorrow."

"Not that different. Not to me. You don't give me much credit, do you?"

He heard the irritation in her voice as she also rose. He knew she didn't like his repeated assurances that her feelings for him were being unduly influenced by what they had been through together—but eventually she would realize that he was right.

He was afraid she was going to argue more. But it seemed even Chloe's impressive courage had limits. "I'll lie down for a while in the small bedroom," she said, turning toward the door. "Let me know if you find anything interesting."

"I will."

He watched her leave. There was wounded pride in the angle of her shoulders when she stepped into the hallway. Maybe she was already getting over her crush, he mused. Maybe she was beginning to remember now why she hadn't much liked him before they'd been forced to spend so much time together.

Picturing the condition of her feet, he grimaced, almost feeling the pain she must have endured. She hadn't deserved any of what she had been through the past few days. He was convinced that Bryan would do everything he could to make certain she would never have to suffer fear or pain again. Chloe deserved to live in luxury.

Donovan still believed Bryan would charm her into marrying him. Bryan had recognized immediately what a special woman she was—perhaps even more quickly than Donovan had. A fitting match for an extraordinary man like Bryan Falcon.

As for himself—well, he was merely ordinary. From his dysfunctional childhood to his occasionally disreputable adulthood, he'd been nobody until Bryan had given him a job—and, more than that, a future.

A future that included her only as his best friend's wife.

He closed his eyes and gave himself a moment to deal with that pain. And then he shoved his feelings aside and turned away from the hallway into which she had disappeared. He had to figure out a way to get them out of here. The sooner, the better.

Chloe was tired, but not sleepy. Lying on top of the quilt that served as a spread on the twin bed in the smaller of the trailer's two bedrooms, she stared at the ceiling and wondered what the next day would bring—as she had been doing for the past half hour or so since she had left Donovan in the living room.

By this time tomorrow, if not before, she could well be back in her own apartment, reunited with her sister, back to her "normal" life. Perhaps trying desperately to pretend that she was still the same person she had been before three greedy and unscrupulous men had ordered her into a van just four days earlier.

She had a bad feeling about the way Donovan had just shut her out after kissing her until she hadn't been able to think of anything but him. About how badly she wanted him. And how hard she had fallen for him.

She knew he still didn't trust their feelings, still felt

torn by his loyalty to Bryan, but she was afraid if they didn't talk while they had the chance, they never would. She would break things off with Bryan, and then Donovan would disappear from her life forever.

She couldn't allow that to happen without even making an effort to stop it. If there was one thing she had learned from this ordeal, it was that sometimes she had to forge ahead despite fear, despite risk, despite the possibility of pain.

She was trying to decide how to confront him about his feelings for her when she heard the outside door to the trailer open and close rather forcefully. Donovan?

She rolled off the bed and hurried toward the main room again.

Donovan was standing just inside the front door to the trailer. His hair was wind-tossed, he was still wearing the ill-fitting flannel shirt and jeans, and he'd found a pair of slip-on canvas shoes that looked a good two sizes too big for him. Anyone else might have looked a bit silly in that garb, she mused, taking a moment to study him. Donovan looked devastatingly sexy—but then, she'd thought the same when he'd been unshaven and dirty and dressed in his ripped black clothes.

His eyebrows lifted when he saw her standing in the doorway. "I'm sorry, did I wake you?"

"I wasn't asleep. What were you doing outside?"

"Just looking around."

"You shouldn't be walking around on that leg. Are you trying to do as much damage to it as possible?"

"I'm trying to get you back to your family," he retorted. "And I found our way out."

Her heart jumped into her throat. "You did? What? How?"

"An ATV. One of the big two-passenger four-wheelers hunters use. It's stored in a small shed out back."

"A locked shed, I presume?"

"It was."

She shook her head. "Did you find a key to the ATV?"

"No. But we won't need one. As soon as you're ready, we'll get on the road."

"You're going to hot-wire it?"

He nodded, apparently having no concern about his ability to do just that.

"We, um, won't be in danger of being arrested for breaking and entering or theft as soon as we reach a town?"

"We aren't stealing anything. We're borrowing—and the owner will be reimbursed for his trouble."

She looked around the trailer, suddenly, unaccountably nervous about leaving it. "What should I do to get ready?"

"Let's try to find you some pants and socks, maybe a pair of shoes. They'll all be too big, of course, but it'll be better than trying to ride on the back of an ATV wearing nothing more than a shirt."

She nodded and turned back toward the bedrooms.

They found her a pair of black sweatpants with a drawstring waist and some thick white tube socks that covered her all the way to her knees. Shoes were more of a problem. They finally uncovered a pair of rubberized lace-up boots that were ridiculously large, but she was able to keep them on by lacing them tightly around her ankles.

"I look ridiculous," she said ruefully, glancing down at her outfit.

As if by impulse, Donovan reached out to smooth a strand of hair away from her face. "You look fine."

Something in his voice made her reach out to him. "Donovan—"

He turned away. "We'd better get going. It's almost 4:00 p.m. now, and we don't know how far we are from a town."

"I know we have to concentrate on getting rescued now," she said evenly, though his rebuff had stung. "But when we get back, we need to talk."

"When we get back, we're both going to be very busy," he replied. "First thing we do is make sure the guys who grabbed us are identified and brought to justice. After that, I've got a week's worth of work to catch up on. I'm going to be tied up for quite a while—as I'm sure you will be."

"And what about us?"

He shrugged, refusing to meet her eyes. "I doubt that we'll see each other much. Except for your connection to Bryan, you and I don't exactly move in the same circles. If you break things off with him, as you say you're thinking about doing, there will be no reason for us to see each other at all."

She bit her lip. He couldn't make his message much clearer. He had every intention of taking her back to civilization and then walking away from her.

"I'll miss you," she said quietly.

His cheek muscles flexed. "You'll get over it."

"I don't think so."

He took a step toward the doorway. "I'll go start the ATV, and bring it around to the front."

"Donovan." It took more courage for her to speak

then than it had to plunge into that forest on the first night, or to face any of the obstacles they had shared since. "What *do* you feel about me?"

He stopped with his back to her, his shoulders tense. "What I feel at this moment isn't really relevant. It's what's waiting for us in our real lives that matters. You have your shop, your sister, your parents—you can have Bryan, if you want him. I have my work. You want to get married, have kids, paint your picket fences. I don't even want a houseplant. Too much responsibility. The thing would die of neglect."

Was it that he didn't want responsibility—or was he afraid of it? He'd survived a father who had walked out on him, a mother who had died of a neglected infection, relatives who apparently hadn't wanted him or cared enough about him, a stint in the military, a bodyguarding assignment that had ended badly. The only stability he'd known in his life had apparently come from his friendship with Bryan.

Understanding his fears didn't help her figure out how to get through them.

Maybe she was reading too much into a few kisses. But she didn't think so. She believed Donovan cared for her. He'd shown her so in too many ways to discount. Now if only she could get him to admit it—first to himself, and then to her.

He didn't give her a chance to argue any further. "I'll bring the ATV around to the front. Meet me there when you're ready to go."

He walked out of the room without looking back.

Pushing away a weary urge to cry, Chloe ran a hand through her hair and tried, in vain, to be more excited about the prospect of rescue.

* * *

"Chloe!"

Looking around in response to her name, Chloe didn't even have a chance to speak before she was engulfed in a hug that nearly cut off her air supply. Instead of protesting, she returned the embrace, as happy as Grace was to be reunited with her twin. The IV line in her right arm got in the way, but they ignored it as they rejoiced in being back together.

Wearing a thin hospital gown to replace the clothes she'd borrowed from the trailer, she was lying in a narrow bed in a northwest Arkansas hospital. She could hardly remember how she'd gotten here. After a teeth-jarring, bone-jolting hour on the back of the noisy ATV, she had been dazed, feverish and exhausted when Donovan had driven them into a small town. The town's tiny police station was one of the first buildings they had spotted. Donovan had driven her straight to the front door.

The next couple of hours had been a blur of activity. Explanations, telephone calls, people hovering over her, bringing her blankets and warm drinks, and finally a long ambulance ride to this hospital, where she and Donovan had been separated immediately. She'd wanted to cling to him, but she'd managed to resist, knowing that he needed medical attention as badly as she did.

It bothered her that he had hardly looked at her as they'd wheeled him away.

She hadn't been in this room long before Grace and Bryan had rushed in. Sitting on the bed beside her, Grace finally pushed back far enough to study her. "Oh, my God, you look awful. Are you all right?"

"The doctor treated some wounds on my feet and

prescribed some strong antibiotics to ward off infection. I was mildly dehydrated, so they hooked up the IV. I'm tired, of course, but I'll be fine.''

"You scared me half to death,'' Grace scolded, lines of strain still visible around her eyes and mouth. "I didn't know if you were alive or hurt or…well, you know.''

"I know. I'm sorry for what you went through.'' Chloe could only imagine how she would have felt if the situation had been reversed.

Having held back until after the sisters' reunion, Bryan approached then, his blue eyes dark with concern. "I'm so sorry about this, Chloe. If I'd had any idea something like this would happen—''

Managing to give him a weary smile, she shook her head against the thin hospital pillow. "It wasn't your fault. Donovan was certain some man named Childers was behind the kidnapping.''

"Donovan was right—as he usually is. Childers hired the men who grabbed you.'' Though he kept his expression pleasant enough, there was a hardness in Bryan's voice that she hadn't heard before.

"And the other three? The men he hired?''

"We have two of them. The other's still at large— but we'll get him.'' His eyes were as hard as his voice now, glittering like polished blue metal.

This was the Bryan Falcon she'd heard about but had never personally encountered, she realized. The ruthless businessman who was as cool as ice in the toughest business crisis, utterly merciless when he was double-crossed. He wore his power like an invisible cloak—not a soldier, but a general who surrounded himself with a small, carefully selected and highly skilled ring of followers.

And yet it was his second-in-command who occupied Chloe's thoughts. Who had captured her heart.

"How is Donovan?" Bryan asked, looking toward the open doorway of her room. "I haven't seen him yet."

She roused herself to answer briskly. "He's having his right leg X-rayed. I'm pretty sure he broke a bone in a fall a couple of days ago. He's been walking on it ever since, so I'm worried that he's done some damage to it."

"What have you been through since Monday evening?" Grace murmured, brushing a strand of hair from Chloe's cheek.

Chloe sighed. "It's a long story."

Bryan pulled up a chair on her other side and took her hand, which had been lying limply next to her. "Is there anything I can do for you now? Anything you want?"

She wanted Donovan. She wanted to be back there with him right now, finding out how he was, holding his hand instead of Bryan's. She couldn't say any of those things, of course. She settled for a wan smile. "I'm okay now. But thank you."

Bryan frowned a little, as if he sensed that something had changed between them. He probably thought she blamed him for what she had been through. She would have to convince him that she didn't blame him in any way, even as she tried to come up with a way to let him know that there was no future for them now.

Some instinct made her look toward the doorway. Braced by a set of metal crutches, Donovan stood there with no expression at all on his face as he looked at her lying there between Grace and Bryan—with Bryan holding her hand.

She pulled her hand quickly from Bryan's. Bryan didn't seem to notice as he stood and moved quickly toward his friend.

"How are you, Donovan?" he asked, and his voice was much warmer now than it had been when he'd spoken of the kidnappers.

"Can't complain," Donovan drawled in response.

Even Chloe had to smile at that. If anyone had a right to complain, it was Donovan. His face was hollow and pale, bruised at the temple and the corner of his mouth. The clothes he'd found at the trailer had been replaced by a set of pale green hospital scrubs, and assorted scrapes and bruises were visible in the V-neckline and beneath the short sleeves. His right leg was encased in a temporary cast from the knee down.

She hadn't seen much of his sense of humor during the past few days, though she'd known from things Bryan had said about him that he had one. According to Bryan, a dry and clever one. She wished she could have gotten to know that side of him better. Not that it would have made her love him any more than she already did. She simply wanted to know every aspect of Donovan.

"They didn't want to hook you up to any tubes and pumps?" Bryan asked him.

Donovan shrugged. "They wanted to. I didn't want them to. I won."

"Big surprise."

Chloe couldn't believe he was just planning to walk out of the hospital—even on crutches. "Aren't you even going to stay overnight?" she fretted. "Surely you need more treatment than a brace and a pair of crutches. Is your leg broken?''

The faint smile he'd worn for Bryan disappeared when he glanced her way. ''They gave me some shots. Some pills to take for a few days. I've cracked a bone in my leg, as we suspected. The local doc patched it up until I can get to an orthopedic specialist.''

Bryan nodded. ''You'll have the best, of course, as soon as we get you back home.''

Chloe remembered Donovan's assertion that he didn't have a home. She hadn't believed him then, nor did she now. He had ties he simply didn't choose to acknowledge. She wondered again if it was apprehension or preference that kept him from doing so.

''You're sure you don't want to spend the night here?'' Bryan asked Donovan. ''It wouldn't hurt you to let someone else take care of you for a few hours.''

Donovan shook his head fiercely. ''I've already had this argument with a couple dozen hospital personnel. I'm not staying. I have things to do. I'll see a doctor in Little Rock tomorrow about the leg.''

''Thick-headed,'' Grace murmured.

Chloe shot her sister a frown. ''Don't start, Grace. Donovan saved my life more times than I can count during the past few days. You should be thanking him.''

Grace studied Chloe's face for a moment, then glanced at Donovan, whose frown had only deepened in response to Chloe's defense. ''In that case, I *will* thank you. With all my heart.''

''Not necessary,'' he said gruffly. ''Just doing my job.''

If he'd been trying to hurt her, he couldn't have done it any better, Chloe thought.

Bryan shook his head. "I'd say you definitely went beyond the call of duty this time, pal. And now you're exhausted. We'd better get on our way. Jason's waiting in the lobby. Grace...?"

"I'd like to stay here with Chloe tonight," Grace answered quickly. "I'll sleep in that recliner."

"That isn't necessary, Grace," Chloe assured her.

Her twin shook her head. "I'm not letting you out of my sight for a couple of days. Besides, you know I don't trust hospitals. Someone has to stay here to make sure you get the proper care."

Chloe was sure the hospital staff would not appreciate Grace's close supervision. Still, she was glad her sister was staying. She didn't want to be left alone with her thoughts tonight.

"We need to get you off your feet," Bryan said to Donovan. "You look like you could fall over in a strong wind."

He approached the bed again and leaned over to press a kiss to Chloe's forehead. "I'll see you in the morning. Have Grace call me if you need anything at all, okay?"

She forced another smile for him. "I will. Thank you, Bryan."

He studied her for another moment, his expression a bit quizzical. And then he turned back to his friend. "Let's go, D.C. You can tell me all about your adventures in the car."

Chloe looked quickly toward Donovan, growing a little panicky at the thought of him walking out that door. She had grown so accustomed to being with him. Their eyes met—and, for only a moment, she thought she saw a similar emotion there, a reluctance to leave her.

And then he turned his head away, speaking to Bryan in a low voice that she couldn't quite hear as they moved out into the hallway together.

He hadn't said goodbye, but Chloe heard it, anyway. As far as Donovan was concerned, it was over between them.

Chapter Fourteen

Surrounded by mirrors of every shape and style, Chloe tried not to pay much attention to her reflection. Her short, artfully choppy hairstyle was flattering, but she'd worn the longer bob so long it still startled her occasionally to catch a glimpse of the new cut. It made her seem like a different person than she had been four weeks ago—but then, she *was* a different person. She'd figured she might as well look it.

Noting that it was ten minutes after closing time, she politely ushered the last browser out of her shop and locked the door behind her. It had been a long, busy day. Good for business, but it had left her tired.

But, then, she was tired a lot these days. She'd found it very difficult to shake the depression that had gripped her since Donovan had walked out of her hospital room.

She had neither seen him nor heard from him since.

Carrying a box of bubble-wrapped pottery candle-sticks, Grace entered from the storeroom and crossed to the shelf where they would be displayed. "Did Mrs. Purvis finally leave?"

"Yeah. I sort of herded her out."

"For someone who spends so much time in here, you would think she'd buy something occasionally."

"She bought that bag of potpourri last month," Chloe reminded her ironically.

"Oh, right. We've made a whole fifty cents off her."

"She's a sweet lady. Just lonely. She likes us, and she loves our mirrors. She just can't bring herself to spend the money for one."

Grace muttered something beneath her breath and set a candlestick on the shelf with a thump.

If Chloe had been depressed during the past month, Grace had been more temperamental than usual. Chloe had chalked it up to lingering anxiety; Grace tended to get snappy when she was stressed or worried, and she had been worried sick about Chloe. But now she was beginning to wonder if there was more to it than that. After all, Chloe had been safe for weeks.

Nor should Grace have to fret any longer about the possibility of Chloe entering an amiable marriage of convenience with Bryan. That was over. Chloe had politely informed Bryan only days after she was rescued that she'd given his offer a great deal of thought and had decided to decline. She had assured him that he shouldn't take the rejection personally; she was very fond of him and thought he would make a wonderful husband and father. Just not with her.

He'd taken the news well, without any sign of disappointment. Either he'd been prepared for her decision or he'd come to the same conclusion. Assuring her that they would remain friends, he had made a polite exit. He'd called two or three times since to check on her and Grace, but their conversations were growing shorter each time.

She didn't think she would be seeing either Bryan or Donovan again.

She had not mentioned her feelings for Donovan to Bryan. Hadn't mentioned Donovan at all, actually, except to politely inquire about his leg, which she had been told was healing satisfactorily. She wouldn't risk causing any problems between Bryan and Donovan, especially since she didn't know whether Donovan had even given her a second thought since he'd brought her out of those woods.

She'd thought he would have at least called her.

"So are you going to stand there gazing out the door the rest of the night, or are you going to help me set out this new shipment?"

Grace's acerbic question brought her attention back to the present. "Sorry. I was distracted."

"You're always distracted these days," Grace muttered.

"And you're always grumpy," Chloe retorted.

Rather than snapping back at her, Grace knelt in front of the display shelf in silence for several long moments, and then she looked up at Chloe with a grimace. "I am, aren't I? I'm sorry."

Chloe could rarely hold a grudge against her twin. "It's okay. I know you've been through a lot lately."

Grace groaned. "That's hardly an excuse, especially since you went through so much more. I just— well, I've been worried about you."

"About me?" Chloe set a yellow-and-blue-patterned candlestick on a shelf, then fussed with its placement for a moment. "There's no need. Bryan has repeatedly promised us that the kidnapping threat is over."

"From what I saw of the weasel Childers, I agree. I thought he was going to faint when Bryan and Jason faced him down in his apartment."

Chloe nodded. "Anyway, now that the publicity has died down and the press has turned its attention to other things, other misfortunate people, I can fade quietly and safely back into obscurity. I'm fine."

Her sister moved to stand beside her, studying her profile. "You're unhappy."

Chloe didn't meet her twin's eyes as she shifted a marble egg into a more conspicuous position. "Of course I'm not un—"

"Chloe." Grace sounded irritated again now. "Please don't try bluffing with me. You know you've never been able to fool me."

Chloe sighed heavily. "You're right. I don't know what's been wrong with me lately. A mild case of post-traumatic stress syndrome, maybe. I'm sure I'll get over it soon."

"I feel like it's my fault."

That comment startled her into turning to stare at Grace. "Your fault? Why on earth would you think that?"

Hanging her head a little, Grace replied, "I think you broke up with Bryan because I made such a fuss about it at the beginning. You had decided you wanted to marry a decent guy and have a family, and I had no right to interfere. I would still rather see you marry for love, but if friendship is more important to you, then that should be all that matters. Bryan's a decent guy. I'm sure he would beef up his security for you if you start seeing him again, so you'd probably be safer than you are just driving to work in the morning now.''

She shook her head impatiently, drew a deep breath and blurted, ''What I'm trying to say is, I think you and Bryan should get back together if it would make you happy again. You should marry him and have those kids you both want so badly. I'll support your decision whole-heartedly.''

For the life of her, Chloe couldn't have explained why tears suddenly gathered in her eyes. ''That's very considerate of you, Grace, but I don't *want* to marry Bryan. As you have pointed out on numerous occasions, I don't love him. I never will.''

Grace looked startled. ''You said yourself that you're very fond of him.''

''I am. Very. But that isn't enough.''

''Since when?''

Since she had fallen passionately and permanently in love with another man, Chloe thought in despair. ''I just changed my mind.''

Grace studied her for a long time, then pushed a hand through her hair. ''Sorry. I would have sworn you've been behaving like a woman with a broken heart.''

Unable to come up with a good response, Chloe turned away.

They worked in silence for a few minutes, with Chloe hoping Grace would change the subject, and Grace apparently lost in her thoughts. It was Grace who broke the silence again. ''When did you talk to Bryan last?''

"He called earlier this afternoon. He said to tell you hello, by the way."

Grace cleared her throat, then asked, "Did he mention how Donovan's doing?"

Just the sound of his name made her chest ache. "He's fine. He's off the crutches, but still in a walking cast."

"Donovan's never called you himself?"

"No."

"That seems a bit odd, doesn't it?"

"I'm sure he knows Bryan is keeping me updated."

"Mm. So I guess you and Donovan didn't become fast friends during your ordeal?"

"No, I suppose we didn't." Because this conversation was entirely too painful, she turned abruptly away. "You can finish this. I'll go close out the register."

Lost in her own thoughts again, Grace didn't reply.

Donovan and Bryan were walking through the lobby of a St. Louis hotel when Donovan was nearly slammed to the floor. It was only Bryan's lightning reflexes that save him from an ignominious fall.

"Whoa, there, buddy." Bryan scooped the runaway three-year-old into his arms only a moment before the child barreled into Donovan's bum leg.

Grateful for the quick save, Donovan glanced around for the kid's parents. There were a lot of people around, but he didn't see anyone who seemed to be looking for the boy.

"Where's your mom?" Bryan asked the child as he set him back on his feet.

The red-haired tot waved an arm vaguely in the direction of the gift shop. "Over there."

"Let's go find her, shall we?"

The boy took Bryan's outstretched hand and nodded obligingly. "'Kay."

It always amazed Donovan how quickly children took to Bryan. That notorious charm of his was as effective with the kids as it was with the ladies.

"I'll be right back if you want to wait here," Bryan said over his shoulder as the boy led him away.

Donovan nodded and moved to one of the deep sofas arranged invitingly around the big, airy lobby. He was sitting there when Bryan rejoined him a few minutes later.

Bryan was still smiling. "Cute kid," he said, taking a chair near Donovan's sofa. "His mother was going nuts looking for him in the gift shop. She says he's worse than Houdini when it comes to making dramatic escapes."

"She needs to put a leash on him. Anyone could have snatched him." The thought of his own recent encounter with kidnappers was enough to make Donovan scowl.

"She said she would watch him more carefully from now on. She seemed like a good mother. She just got distracted for a minute."

Donovan watched as Bryan looked toward the gift shop again, and something in his friend's eyes made him ask, "You still want kids, don't you?"

Bryan seemed startled by the question—which, admittedly, *was* more personal than Donovan usually got—but he answered candidly, "Yeah. I've always thought I'd make a pretty good father, even though my own was hardly a role model."

"I think you would, too."

"Thanks for the vote of confidence."

Donovan waited as long as he could before saying reluctantly, "Chloe would make a good mother."

Again, Bryan's eyebrows shot up in an expression of surprise, probably because Donovan had hardly mentioned Chloe's name in the past month. "Yes, I thought she would, too. That was one of the reasons why I decided she and I would make a good match. Obviously, I was wrong about that part."

"You didn't fight for her very hard. When she broke it off, you just let her go."

"And what was I supposed to do?" Bryan asked dryly. "Lock her up?"

"You should have been patient. You knew she was still suffering from shock when we came out of those woods, but you let her break it off only a few days later. If you'd hung in there, been there for her, comforted her, tried to make it all up to her, she would have come around."

"I don't think so."

Donovan didn't know why he was pushing this—hell, he should be glad he wouldn't have to deal with watching Bryan and Chloe together—but for some reason he felt he had to say it.

He was very fond of both Bryan and Chloe, he told himself, feeling a bit noble for his unselfishness. He didn't like the thought of either of them being alone, unsatisfied. "Maybe you should give it another try."

Bryan sighed. "To be honest, I'm not sure I want to give it another try. I like and admire Chloe a great deal. I think she's amazing—brave, resourceful, intelligent. I just don't think I want to marry her."

Donovan couldn't believe what he was hearing. "Why the hell not?"

"I don't know," Bryan answered, a bit defensively now. "Maybe Grace was right. I was thinking about marrying Chloe for the wrong reasons. Respect and admiration aren't synonymous with love."

Shaking his head in disgust, Donovan muttered, "Grace is hardly one to be giving romantic advice. From what I saw, she's a spitfire."

"Grace isn't so bad. She just genuinely wants what's best for Chloe. And so do I. Chloe deserves to find someone who'll love her and treat her right."

"I can't imagine she would find anyone who would treat her better than you would."

"I'm touched."

"I'm beginning to believe that you are," Donovan muttered. "Look all you want for the perfect match, but you aren't going to find anyone better than Chloe."

Bryan chuckled. "Hell, D.C., if you feel that way about her, why don't *you* marry her?"

To his chagrin, Donovan felt a wave of heat rise from the collar of his crisp white shirt. He looked away quickly, pretending interest in a silicone-busted blonde who was mincing past them, making an obvious play to get their attention. "As you said," he muttered, "Chloe deserves the best."

He was aware that Bryan was watching him closely, but he refused to look around. "We'd better get moving again," he said, pushing himself off the sofa. "We don't want to be late for the meeting."

Feeling like a complete idiot, he headed toward the elevators.

This was what he got for trying to do something

nice for two people he cared about, he thought irritably. He'd made such a botch of it that he had been
left looking like a fool. God only knew what Bryan
was thinking right now. He should have just stayed
out of it—but he'd had an irrational hope that getting
Bryan and Chloe back together might help him get
her out of his mind. Out of his dreams.

Out of his heart, damn it.

He should have known better.

Bryan was sitting in his Little Rock office a couple
of days later when the intercom on his desk buzzed.
"Mr. Falcon? Ms. Pennington is on line two. Are you
available to take her call?"

He looked up from the paperwork in front of him.
"Yes, thanks, Marta."

He picked up the receiver. "Good morning, Chloe.
Is everything all right?"

"It isn't Chloe, it's Grace."

That made him sit back in his chair, his eyebrows
rising sharply. "Grace? What is it? What's happened?"

He couldn't imagine that Chloe's sister would be
calling him unless something was terribly wrong.

"No, everything's okay. I just need to ask you a
question."

He relaxed—a little. A call from Grace Pennington
was still fraught with peril. "What question do you
want to ask me?"

"How's Donovan?"

This call was becoming more intriguing all the
time, Bryan thought, settling more comfortably into
his chair. Perhaps he and Grace had been on the same

wavelength recently—definitely an astonishing thought. "Why do you ask?"

"I still don't know why you were so insistent that we needed to spend the day at the river house," Chloe announced as she sat in her sister's car one Wednesday morning in early June, watching Grace drive. "I really had quite a few things to do today."

"I told you," Grace replied, "I just needed to get away for a day and I didn't want to come by myself."

Grace *had* been working awfully hard lately, Chloe conceded. And she did seem in need of a vacation; she had been so tense and stressed.

"I'm surprised Mom and Dad didn't want to come, too. They love to spend the day with us at the river."

"Mom had that garden club thing this afternoon," Grace reminded her.

Chloe sat back in the leather bucket seat of Grace's two-seater, which bumped a bit roughly over the rural roads that led to their parents' vacation cabin on the Little Red River. It had been quite a while since she'd made this trip. She'd been too busy before the kidnapping, and since then she'd been avoiding any reminders of vacation homes and woods and lakes and rivers—anything that made her think of the time she had spent with Donovan.

But she couldn't spend the rest of her days hiding from her memories. She had to get on with her life—and she supposed this was as good a time as any to get started.

It was obvious that their parents had been to the river house recently, she noted when Grace drove onto the long gravel driveway. Their mother's flower beds had been watered and weeded, and the many windows in the two-story log cabin had been washed until they sparkled in the bright sunlight. A large porch lined with swings and rockers and cooled by old-fashioned ceiling fans hinted of lazy summer days spent relaxing and watching the river roll by.

She smiled at the memory of cookouts with her family, trout-fishing with her dad and sleepovers with her sister and their friends in the loft bedroom. She'd spent a lot of happy times here; why had she been so reluctant to come today?

"Maybe this *was* a good idea," she admitted.

Grace flashed her a smile. "Didn't I tell you so? It's our slowest day at work, so Bob and Justin can handle everything there. You and I can just chill out."

"I can't wait to get into my waders. It's been so long since I've had a fly rod in my hands I've probably forgotten how to cast."

"Oh, I doubt that. I have a feeling you'll definitely catch something today."

Chloe had to smile at Grace's wording. "A cold, probably."

"Cute." Grace parked the car and opened her door. "Grab the groceries, will you? I'll carry the drinks."

They had come prepared to grill hamburgers later. Grace had brought so much food that Chloe had accused her of buying enough for half a dozen people instead of just two. Grace had merely shrugged and claimed she'd gotten carried away.

The inside of the house had not changed since Chloe had last visited. They entered into a two-story-high main room with a large rock fireplace and a ceiling fan with a light fixture overhead. To the back of the main room, separated by a low dining bar, was the kitchen and dining room combination. The master bedroom opened off the other side of the living room, beneath the stairs. Upstairs, a loft sitting room overlooked the living room, and two small bedrooms shared another bath. One entire side of the house consisted of large windows that overlooked the river.

The log walls were hung with duck prints and primitive art, the furnishing were worn and comfortable, the wooden floors warmed by thick braided rugs. Chloe always thought of her parents' weekend hideaway as a nap waiting to happen.

She carried the groceries into the kitchen and deposited them on a tile countertop, stowing perishables in the refrigerator. Returning to the main room, she found Grace peering out a window toward the driveway. "Expecting someone?"

Grace jumped, looking almost comically guilty. "Of course not," she said, her voice oddly breathless. "Why do you ask?"

Eyeing her twin curiously, Chloe shook her head. "You *do* need a day off, don't you? You're as jumpy as a cat."

"I told you, I've been working too hard."

"Apparently. So, what do you want to do first? It's too early to start the grill. We could fish."

"You know, I think I'd rather just rest for a while. I brought a new mystery, so I think I'll curl up in a rocker and read for a couple hours."

"Okay. I'll go fish by myself. You always scare the trout away, anyway."

"I don't always scare them away. I just get mad sometimes when I hook one and then lose it."

Chloe grinned as she pictured Grace stamping her feet in the water and throwing rocks at the fish that got away. She never actually hit one of them, of course, but she guaranteed that no one else would catch any, either. "Enjoy your book. I'll see you later."

"Mm," Grace murmured behind her. "Much later."

Deciding she would never figure out her twin's odd mood, Chloe headed out to the storeroom where her father kept the fishing gear.

"Tell me again why you want to buy another vacation cabin?" Donovan asked Bryan quizzically, watching cornfields, cow pastures and mobile homes pass by outside the passenger window of Bryan's car.

Sitting behind the wheel, Bryan glanced away from the road ahead to reply, "I've gotten tired of the place in Missouri. Bad memories there now. I'd like to find someplace smaller and easier to get to. The cabin you and I are visiting sounds ideal."

"So why do you need me here? You don't require my approval to buy anything."

"I just wanted company, okay? And I do value your opinion."

Donovan shrugged. "Then I'm happy to oblige."

A small red sports car passed them going the opposite direction. It was driven by a woman in large sunglasses and a floppy hat, both of which concealed her face. Donovan told himself it was a depressing clue to his state of mind that the woman still looked like Chloe to him.

Sometimes he saw her everywhere he looked.

Bryan's cell phone buzzed. He sighed heavily, reached into his pocket, and held the small device to his ear. "Falcon."

Donovan gazed out the window as Bryan carried

on a brief, monosyllabic conversation. And then Bryan disconnected the call and brought Donovan out of his morose musings with an exclamation of satisfaction. "Ah. This is the cabin, I think. Nice, isn't it?"

Donovan studied the neat log cabin in front of them. A pleasant place—well-tended flower beds, a big, inviting porch, nice river view—but it was hardly as luxurious as Bryan's vacation home in Missouri. That one obviously belonged to a very wealthy man; this one looked like a middle-class weekend cottage. There wasn't even a security system, as far as he could tell.

"It has potential, I guess," he said to Bryan. "You could probably put a gate at the end of this driveway, maybe fence the boundaries of the lot."

"Turn this pretty place into a fortress? That would be a shame, don't you think?"

"I think a man in your position has to be more concerned about security than the average fisherman—as you should know very well by now," Donovan retorted.

"Ever since Childers went nuts and implemented that crazy kidnapping plan, you've been more protective than an old nanny," Bryan scolded indulgently. "Might I remind you that Jason is my security chief, not you?"

"So why isn't he with you today?"

"Because I want the opinion of a friend, not a paid advisor."

Though this whole plan still seemed impulsive and illogical to Donovan, he decided to humor his friend for now. "Okay, let's go check the place out. You have a key?"

"Of course."

As Donovan followed Bryan into the cabin, he was reminded again of middle-income suburbia. No professional decorator had stepped foot through these doors. The furnishings and decor looked as though they'd been assembled during years of family vacations and long weekends. Some of his and Bryan's wealthy friends would have turned up their noses in scorn at what they would have considered such primitive accommodations—but Donovan rather liked it. It was...comfortable. Inviting. Homey.

Bryan rubbed the back of his neck as he looked around. "Nice," he murmured, "but I don't know if it's exactly what I have in mind."

If Bryan decided he didn't want the place, Donovan thought he might consider buying it himself. He didn't have to worry about security as much as Bryan—not usually, anyway. And while he hadn't been in the habit of taking leisurely weekends away from work before now, he'd been considering making some changes in his routines. A man needed something besides work in his life, he had recently concluded. Maybe he should take up fishing.

He wandered to the far side of the room, looking out through the wall of glass there. "There's a rock walkway that leads down to the river."

"Why don't you check it out while I look around a bit more in here?" Bryan suggested. "I'll join you down by the river shortly."

Bryan must have sensed that he was feeling drawn to the river. He nodded and reached for the handle of the French doors that led out onto a big wooden deck.

"Donovan."

He paused and looked over his shoulder. "Yes?"

"Sometimes decisions have to be made with the heart, not the head, to be right. Keep that in mind, will you?"

Frowning, Donovan blurted, "What the hell are you talking about?"

"Just remember what I said." Bryan's smile looked a little smug and just a bit wistful. "Go on down to the river. I'll see you later."

Closing the door behind him, Donovan shook his head as he carefully descended the steps to the rock walkway. He still wore a walking cast, but it was hidden beneath his loose slacks and he'd gotten used to getting around in it.

As he walked, he wondered if Bryan could be going through some sort of midlife crisis, though thirty-eight seemed a bit early for midlife. He had done and said some strange things lately, leaving Donovan struggling to keep up. What was that stuff about making decisions with the heart? Was he talking about this place? Pointing out that sometimes a decision felt right even when it didn't seem logical? If Bryan wanted to buy this cabin despite the drawbacks, Donovan certainly wouldn't try to stop him.

Someone was standing beside the river on the other side of a stand of trees that had blocked the view from the cabin. It was a woman, dressed in a pink tank top beneath suspendered fishing waders, standing with her back to him. A floppy hat covered her short hair, and a fly rod lay on the ground beside her, although she wasn't fishing at the moment. She was just standing there, looking out at the water, seemingly lost in her thoughts.

She, too, looked like Chloe, he thought with a scowl. He really was seeing her everywhere.

He was just about to turn around and leave her to her privacy when she suddenly knelt down, picked up a stone and threw it at the water. It was an obvious attempt to skip the rock across the water—but the angle was all wrong. The rock sank with a splash.

The woman's exasperated mutter carried on a soft breeze to where he stood.

His hands clenched into fists at his sides. "Chloe," he said, hardly aware that he'd said her name aloud.

She froze, then jerked around to face him, her eyes wide beneath the brim of her floppy fishing hat. "Donovan! What are you doing here?"

Chapter Fifteen

Chloe couldn't believe Donovan was standing there on her parents' walkway, looking at her as though she had materialized from thin air in front of him. Her first instinct was to run toward him, to throw herself into his arms. But he looked so stern and stiff that she wasn't entirely sure he would catch her if she did.

"What are you doing here?" she asked again when he didn't answer the first time.

"I was just about to ask you the same question."

She tilted her head curiously. "You didn't know I was here?"

"I had no idea."

He looked wonderful, she couldn't help noticing as she tried to process his words. His hair looked freshly cut—though that recalcitrant lock still fell forward on his forehead—and the dark hollows of pain were gone from his clean-shaven face. His left foot was encased in a leather slip-on shoe, and his right foot was wrapped in a cast designed for walking. He wore a designer shirt and crisply tailored chinos, but he had looked just as good to her in the ill-fitting garments he'd borrowed from that trailer. "I still don't understand why you're here."

"I came with Bryan. He's thinking about buying this place."

That made her frown deepen. "This place isn't for sale. It belongs to my parents."

"Your parents?" Donovan looked as confused as she was now. "Are you sure they don't want to sell it?"

"I'm positive. They would have told me if they were. They knew Grace and I were coming here today—they certainly would have mentioned if it was for sale."

"Grace is here, too?" Donovan looked around as if he expected to see her twin lurking behind a tree nearby.

"She's in the house. Didn't you see her?"

"No. Bryan and I were just in the house. Bryan let us in with a key. No one was there."

"Bryan has a key to my parents' vacation house?" This situation was getting stranger by the minute. "I think we'd better go find out what's going on."

Donovan nodded. "I think you're right."

She bent to pick up her fly rod. She hadn't been in the mood to fish, anyway. She'd spent the time since she'd walked down here gazing at the water and thinking about Donovan. And then to turn and see him standing there—as if her thoughts had conjured him—well, she was still half in shock.

He waited for her to pass him. She noticed as he

followed her that he was walking well, hardly limping at all despite the cast. She couldn't stop looking at him, though she tried to be subtle about it. Yet every time she shot a glance at him, she found him looking back at her as if he was also having trouble looking away.

Reaching the back deck of the house, she propped her rod against the railing, then unlaced and removed her waterproof boots. She unbuckled the belt and suspenders of her stocking-foot waders, and peeled off the shapeless garment to reveal the pink tank top and denim shorts. She was entirely too aware of Donovan watching her every move. She felt as self-conscious as if she were doing a striptease for him, though fishing waders and denim shorts hardly qualified as sexy clothing.

She'd left a pair of pink flip-flops lying beside a chair on the deck; she slipped her feet into them and opened the French doors that led into the house. "Grace?" she called out as she entered with Donovan on her heels.

The house was eerily quiet. Obviously empty. She frowned. "That's odd. Maybe they're on the front porch."

She crossed the main room rapidly and opened the front door. Not only were there no people on the porch, but there were no cars in the driveway. No sign of Grace's two-seater. "Where in the world—?"

"Does Grace drive a red sports car, by any chance?" Donovan asked as she slowly closed the front door and turned to face him.

"Yes. Why?"

"Damn. That's who called him."

"Called who?"

"Bryan." Placing a hand to the back of his neck, he rested his other hand on his hip and gave her a faint, wry smile. "I hate to tell you this, Chloe, but I think we've been kidnapped again."

She gaped at him for a moment, then ran a hand through her disheveled hair, dislodging the fishing hat she was still wearing. She hardly even noticed as it fell to the floor at her feet. "Either my brain isn't working very well today, or everyone is behaving very strangely. I don't understand what's going on."

"You've cut your hair."

She dropped her hand in response to his unexpected comment. "Yes. Grace says I chopped it off."

"I like it."

"Thank you." She motioned toward the couches arranged for conversation around the fireplace. "Sit down. See if you can explain to me what's going on. I assume you've figured it out?"

"I think so."

He waited for her to be seated, and then he sat on the same couch, though at the other end. He turned to face her. "I didn't realize Grace and Bryan had stayed in touch since you and I got back."

"As far as I know, they haven't. I've spoken with Bryan a few times, but the only time he mentioned Grace was when he would tell me to say hi to her for him. And I certainly can't imagine that she would have conspired with him for anything like this."

"Obviously, she did. Uh, Bryan can be impulsive sometimes. Especially when something amuses him."

"So can Grace. It's never easy to predict what she's going to do. But this…"

Because it still made no sense to her, Chloe's thoughts drifted from Grace's strange behavior. She studied Donovan's face, thinking there was some slight difference in his expression, and trying to decide what it was. "I thought you might call me after we returned to our homes. I was disappointed that you didn't," she admitted.

His mouth pulled a bit at one corner. "I didn't want to intrude on your life. And I wasn't sure you'd want to be reminded of what you went through with me."

She shook her head. "That wouldn't have been a problem. I haven't been able to stop thinking about those days we spent together."

"Neither have I."

His low admission gave her the courage to say, "I've missed you, Donovan."

He looked down at his hands. "You certainly didn't waste any time breaking things off with Bryan. I would have thought you'd have given it a little more time."

"I didn't need any more time. I knew there was no future between us. I told you so in that forest, though you didn't seem to believe me at the time."

"I believed you. I just thought—"

"I know. You thought I'd been so traumatized by the ordeal that I couldn't think straight. That my poor little nerves had been overwrought."

He gave her a chiding glance in response to her sarcasm—but at least he was looking at her. "I didn't think that, exactly. I just thought you needed more time for Bryan to convince you what a great guy he is."

"I didn't *need* to be convinced of that. Bryan is a terrific guy. A real prince. And he deserves someone better than me."

Donovan scowled. "That's bull. He could never find anyone better than you."

Locking her hands in her lap, Chloe hoped her instincts about Donovan's feelings were right. If not, she was on the verge of making a fool of herself. Not to mention the fact that she was about to risk a very painful rejection.

Despite the enormous stakes, she managed to speak evenly. "You say you want the best for Bryan. Would you honestly want him to marry someone who's desperately in love with his best friend?"

Donovan went so still he could have been carved from marble. She wasn't even sure he breathed for the next minute or two.

Her fingers clenched so tightly the knuckles ached when she spoke again. "You said my feelings would change when we were out of that forest and back in our real lives. You were wrong. I still feel the same way."

His jaw clenched as he slowly shook his head. "I'm not the kind of man you've been looking for. I've never wanted marriage or kids."

"You didn't want them—or you never thought you would have them because of the bad experiences of your past?" she countered.

"Same difference."

"No. Not even similar."

"You deserve better," he muttered, his usually bright-green eyes dark with suppressed emotion.

"I deserve the same thing Bryan does," she whispered. "Someone who loves me."

She watched his throat work with a hard swallow.

"I asked you once how you felt about me," she reminded him again, her tone very gentle now. "You said it wasn't relevant then. I think it *is* relevant now. How do you feel about me, Donovan?''

His voice was so low she could hardly hear him. ''I've never been in love. I'm not even sure I know what the word means. But I know you haven't been out of my thoughts for one minute since I left you. I know I've never met any woman I admired or respected more. I know I want you so badly my teeth ache. I wake up every night in a cold sweat, aching for you. Missing you.''

Tears were running down her cheeks now. Tears of joy. Of relief. Of hope. And of sympathy, because this was obviously so difficult for him. ''That's close enough.''

He held up a hand. ''I also know that it would kill me if I hurt you or let you down. I don't ever want to see you suffer again. I don't ever want to cause you pain. But I'm afraid I will, because I don't know how the hell to go about making a woman happy. I can give you things—my association with Bryan has made me very comfortable financially—but I know that isn't enough for you.''

She dashed a hand against her cheek. ''No. If money and material things were enough to make me happy, I would have married Bryan. But you're right, it takes a lot more than that to make me happy.''

''And you think you can be happy with me?'' He sounded as though that concept was almost impossible for him to believe.

She couldn't resist reaching out to touch his hard cheek. ''I know I will. And I know I can make you happy, too, if you'll let me.''

Catching her hand, he pressed his lips to her palm in a hard caress that made her heart trip. ''There are people who would say you're crazy to choose me over Bryan.''

''I don't care what anyone says. In my opinion, I've chosen the best man. I love you, Donovan.''

He pulled her into his arms, his mouth crushing hers in a kiss that said everything he couldn't put into words. Sheer poetry, she decided, happily losing herself in the embrace.

''How long do you think Bryan and Grace will stay away?'' she murmured against his lips.

''I don't expect to see them for awhile.'' He brushed his fingers experimentally through her short hair, seemed to like the feeling and did it again. ''Why—do you want to go fishing?''

She gave him a look. ''Now is not the time to start teasing me,'' she informed him, breaking away from his arms to stand and offer him her hand. ''You can prove that you really do have a sense of humor after you make love with me.''

''Are you going to be a demanding sort of wife?'' he asked as he rose to stand beside her.

Wife. The word shot through her like an arrow. Was this Donovan's idea of a proposal?

She swallowed before answering lightly, ''Yes, I'm going to be very high-maintenance. You're going to have to spend the rest of your life catering to my whims.''

He pretended to give her warning a moment's thought, and then he nodded. ''I can live with that.''

Apparently, they were engaged.

So the man she loved wasn't exactly the most romantic or silver-tongued charmer in the world. She didn't care. She adored him exactly the way he was.

Smiling like an idiot, Chloe led him up the stairs

toward the bedroom that had always been hers. He stopped at the top of the stairs to kiss her half sense-less again.

"There's only one problem," he murmured, his hands already exploring her curves. "I didn't come prepared for this. I know you want kids, but..."

She broke away with a shaky laugh, feeling as though her skin was melting everywhere he'd touched. "Wait right here," she ordered, and dashed into Grace's room, where she rummaged through a nightstand drawer, emerging with a couple of plastic packets she had suspected she would find there.

She returned triumphantly to Donovan. "I do want children," she assured him, leading him into the other bedroom. "But not quite yet."

Being the gentleman that he was, he didn't ask any questions about the conveniently appearing condoms. She would tell him another time about Grace's broken engagement, and the weekends Grace had once spent here with the man she had planned to marry—but for now, she concentrated only on her own engagement. One that she was certain would end much more hap-pily than her twin's had.

Finally closed into the small, early-American-furnished bedroom with the slanted roof and day-dream-tempting window seat, Donovan turned to pull her back into his arms. It didn't take him long to rid her of her tank top and shorts, nor the flimsy bra and panties she had worn beneath. He growled approval of the skin he'd revealed, his fingers exploring her so slowly and so skillfully that he soon brought her to shivering incoherence by his touch alone.

She helped him remove his own clothes, though her hands were shaking so hard she fumbled more than she assisted. She had never wanted anyone more than she wanted Donovan now. She had never ached, never burned like this. When he finally stood in front of her, naked except for the short cast below his right knee, she saw to her utter delight that he had a powerful ache for her, too.

She reached for him, drawing him slowly against her. Her breath caught when they finally stood skin-to-skin. He groaned.

His hands cupped her bottom, drew her tightly against his rock-hard arousal. She rubbed against him, knowing she was playing with fire, but loving the tremor that ran through him in response. Donovan's control was so formidable that it gave her a heady sense of feminine power to know she had the ability to break through it.

He tumbled her to the bed, falling with her, his mouth locked with hers. She ran her hands over as much of him as she could reach, loving the hard, hot, pulsing strength of him. He didn't wait for her assistance with the protection she'd found for him. He donned it swiftly and with a skill that bespoke experience she wouldn't think about right now.

And then he made her incapable of thinking at all by thrusting so deeply into her that she fancied they would never be completely separate again. He'd made them one—physically, emotionally, permanently.

"I love you, Donovan," she whispered, wrapping herself around him.

"I love you, too," he murmured, his mouth against hers. "This has to be love. It's too much to be anything else."

That made her cry. And then he made her soar.

She'd known since those days in the forest that

they were a perfect match. Together, there were no obstacles they could not overcome.

She'd been looking for a partner. She had found a mate. Now she understood the difference.

They had been recuperating in each other's arms for a long time when they were disturbed by the buzz of Donovan's cell phone, which he'd set on the nightstand when he'd removed the clip from his belt.

"Ignore it," he said when Chloe reached for it.

She shook her head and handed him the small plastic phone, her smile so drowsily satisfied that he almost threw the phone aside and fell onto her again. "It's probably Bryan. You really should talk to him."

Though he sighed, he held the phone to his ear. "What?"

"I was just wondering if you need a ride any time soon," Bryan said without bothering to identify himself. "Or if you're still speaking to me."

"I won't be needing a ride for a while. And I'll have plenty to say to you later," Donovan growled in response.

"How's Chloe?"

"Chloe is fine," Donovan replied, nuzzling against her temple, enjoying the way her newly short hair tickled his cheek. She murmured her pleasure and pressed a kiss to his throat.

"Grace and I thought the two of you needed to talk. Knowing how stubborn you can be, I thought this might be the only way to convince you."

"Mm. From now on, let me make my own moves." He shifted against the sheets as Chloe's hand wandered over his stomach and then dipped downward.

"I'll do that. So, um, things are working out between the two of you?"

"Let's just put it this way. Chloe took your advice about making a choice with her heart instead of her head."

"I always said Chloe was a remarkable woman."

Donovan cleared his throat, trying to read the underlying expression in his friend's voice. "Uh—Bryan..."

"If ever I've seen two people who were more right for each other, it's you and Chloe. It just took us all a while to realize it. Do yourself a favor, D.C. Let yourself be happy for a change."

Bryan disconnected the call before Donovan could come up with a response.

"Bryan and Grace as matchmakers," Chloe murmured, shaking her head. "It's very bizarre."

Donovan was rather dazed by the image, as well. "What I can't figure out is how they knew the way we feel about each other. Unless you said something...?"

"I didn't say anything," she assured him. "And since I sincerely doubt that you did, either, we must have been more transparent to the people who care most about us than we thought."

"Apparently." He hesitated a moment, then asked slowly, "You, uh, are still going to marry me, aren't you?"

She looked at him quizzically. "Did you think I would suddenly change my mind?"

"Well..."

She sighed. "I can tell it's going to take me a while to convince you that I'm very certain of what I'm doing this time. I've reminded you on numerous occasions that I never told Bryan I would marry him, because I sensed that it wasn't right. And I never even pretended to love him. This time I have no doubts. I love *you*."

Donovan told himself he was going to have to start believing her sometime—even though it still seemed incredible to him that Chloe had chosen him over Bryan. And he did believe her…but he figured a little more convincing wouldn't hurt.

"Since we're stranded here for a while longer," he murmured, gathering her close again.

"We might as well make good use of our time," she finished for him, lifting her mouth to his.

"Exactly what I was thinking."

"See?" she asked, just before they both lost the ability to speak. "We're the perfect match, after all."

* * * * *

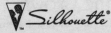

Coming in May 2002

**Three Bravo men marry for convenience—
but will they love in leisure? Find out in
Christine Rimmer's *Bravo Family Ties*!**

Cash—for stealing a young woman's innocence, and to
give their baby a name, in *The Nine-Month Marriage*

Nate—for the sake of a codicil in his beloved
grandfather's will, in *Marriage by Necessity*

Zach—for the unlucky-in-love rancher's chance to
have a marriage—even of convenience—
with the woman he *really* loves!

BRAVO
FAMILY TIES

Where love comes alive™

Visit Silhouette at www.eHarlequin.com   BR3BFT

If you enjoyed what you just read,
then we've got an offer you can't resist!

Take 2 bestselling love stories FREE!

Plus get a FREE surprise gift!

When California's most talked about dynasty is threatened, only family, privilege and the power of love can protect them!

THE COLTONS

Coming in May 2002

THE HOPECHEST BRIDE

by
Kasey Michaels

Cowboy Josh Atkins is furious at Emily Blair, the woman he thinks is responsible for his brother's death...so *why* is he so darned attracted to her? After dark accusations—and sizzling sparks—start to fly between Emily and Josh, they both realize that they can make peace...and love!

Available at your favorite retail outlet.

Silhouette®
Where love comes alive™

Visit Silhouette at www.eHarlequin.com   PSCOLT12